The House at the Center of the Worlds

Books by Scott Reeves

The Big City
Demonspawn
Billy Barnaby's Twisted Christmas
The Dream of an Ancient God
The Last Legend
Inferno: Go to Hell
Scruffy Unleashed: A Novella
Colony
A Hijacked Life
The Dawkins Delusion
The Newer New Revelations
Apocalyptus Interruptus
Death to Einstein!
The House at the Center of the Worlds
The Miracle Brigade
Tales of Science Fiction
Tales of Fantasy
The Chronicles of Varuk: Book One
The Compleat Snowybrook Inn
Liberal vs. Conservative: A Novella
A Crackpot's Notebook, Volume 1
Flames of the Sun

Graphic Novels

Billy Barnaby's Twisted Christmas
The Adventures of Captain Bob in Outer Space

The House at the Center of the Worlds

Scott Reeves

The House at the Center of the Worlds

ISBN-13:
978-1492322528

ISBN-10:
1492322520

The Storm and the Hobo Code

He was walking down a narrow one-lane road that wound through the hilly, deeply wooded back-country. The road was peppered with potholes and cracks. Obviously it didn't get enough traffic to warrant frequent maintenance. He hadn't seen a house for miles, and no cars had passed for hours. The sky had been a leaden gray all afternoon, with pregnant, dark clouds smothering close to the ground and distant flashes of lightning flickering at the far reaches of his vision. The storm finally hit shortly after four, the clouds giving birth to a torrential downpour that pelted him with fat, cold drops which exploded against him with relentless fury. His clothing was quickly drenched. The road soon became a shallow river, and he waded upstream, hunkering beneath the partial shelter afforded him by the heavy backpack that weighed him down, his dripping eyes searching for more permanent shelter.

The trees to either side of the road were an impenetrable wall in the sudden gloomy, wet murk. No hope of shelter there. As he trudged along, his shoes sloshing and squishing through the current, he vainly searched for some opening in the woods, perhaps a private road leading back to a house where he might beg the owner to allow him to wait out the storm on a porch or in a barn.

But there was nothing for nearly half a mile, just the treacherously slick road underfoot and the unyielding woods to either side.

And then, on the thick bole of a gnarly oak, he saw carved a circle with an arrow pointing to the right. Hobo code, "This Way."

Just beyond the carved oak, there was a narrow gap in the trees, and a gravel road leading off to the right, deeper into the trees. He stopped to peer down the side road, his eyebrows dripping a curtain of water, but saw nothing indicative of civilization, just the road swallowed by the mysterious shadows of the deep woods. If there was shelter to be had that way, it must be far back from the county road he'd been following.

Trusting to the hobo code, he hitched his backpack tighter, and started down the gravel way. Immediately the canopy of the trees closed above him to block the brunt of the storm, allowing through only a drippy, tolerable spattering of rain. But the mitigation of the storm came at the cost of light: even back out on the road, the late afternoon light had all but faded into the murky storm; now, he trudged through a darkness that might as well have been night.

He supposed he could have stopped right there and made camp. But if there were a house at the end of this gravel road, he would much prefer the shelter of a barn, or perhaps the warmth of some kind farmer's spare bed. So he continued slogging along, shivering as the wet clothes plastered to his body absorbed the rapidly cooling air of the approaching evening.

The gravel road soon became overgrown with grass and shrubs, so that he found himself following what amounted to little more than a foot path through the gloom of the woods, pushing through briars whose thorns tugged at his clothing as he passed, as if trying to claw him back, away from whatever might be at the end of the trail.

But he pushed on, and the rain increased. It rattled against the leafy canopy above him with a wet, incessant rat-tat-tat, as if something beyond the woods in the waxing night were shooting at him and only the trees were protecting him from the vast and impersonal malice of nature. He picked up his pace, determined to find shelter before the trees finally failed him. Mud had made the trail slick and treacherous, but he slipped and slid through it without a thought for the twisted ankle that was likely to be the result of such carelessness. The darkness was nearly complete, save for the occasional flicker of lightning that somehow managed to penetrate the canopy, briefly revealing the surrounding woods, so that he only had a strobe-like awareness of his passage through the trees. Thunder boomed, jarring his bones and rumbling across the land.

Abruptly, the trail let out into a meadow. He was only aware of it because the rain suddenly pelted him with great ferocity, no longer blocked by the intervening leaves and branches. At the exact moment he stepped into the meadow, a tremendous flash of lightning momentarily dispelled the stormy murk, just long enough to reveal a building at the center of the meadow. A stately Victorian mansion that seemed to be a combination of the Second Empire and Stick styles, both of which he was familiar with due to a brief stint as an architectural major during the aimless years he'd spent wandering the halls of academia in his youth. The grand, sprawling old building had several bay windows on the ground floor and oriel windows on the upper, with a hexagonal tower on the west end that was topped with a tall spire. And soaring above it all was a magnificent central clock tower. The hands on the clock had frozen at four o'clock. The whole structure was sagging with age, and was covered with creeping vines and ivy and sheets of moss that oozed down the sides of the house like a slow green waterfall. It was eerie, happening upon such a place in the backwoods of the world.

In that brief instant of lightning, his eyes fastened on the porch that wrapped around the front and sides of the aged manor house. It beckoned to him, offering shelter from the storm.

He stopped in his tracks at the edge of the woods and waited for the momentary lightning-induced blindness to fade. When he could see once again, he shivered uncontrollably and hunkered in on himself as he studied the place for signs of life. Black clouds still filled the sky, blotting out the last light of the day, but there was still enough that he could just make out the sprawling mansion, squatting there at the center of the meadow.

He thought it was the most beautiful structure he had ever seen. An air of forgotten history and age was soaked into its timbers more deeply even than the rain. There were no lights aglow in the windows, and no noticeable movement anywhere. The place seemed abandoned, but he couldn't imagine anyone abandoning a mansion such as this. There were signs of decay all about it, such as the sagging lines of the various slopes of the roof, and glaringly naked spots where slate shingles were missing. But it still seemed livable, especially to someone such as he, who currently had no home at all.

He crept across the meadow, dogged by the darkness and the rain, keeping a wary eye on the grand mansion. In deep back-country such as he was traversing, people would be quick to pull a gun to protect their own, and he didn't want to be done in by some frightened widow, or a suspicious farmer or his unruly lad who just liked taking potshots at strangers. He of course was not someone to fear, but whoever lived here, if anyone did, would not know that.

But no one responded to his approach as he slogged through the ankle-high, rain-bent grass. He came upon a cobblestone walkway whose stony joints bristled with weeds. The walkway simply began at a random point about fifty feet from the house, and led up to the railed stairs of the porch. Perhaps there had once been a driveway at the end of the cobblestones, but if there once had been, there was no evidence of it now.

He followed the walkway. Belatedly he thought to raise his arms, palms out, hoping to disarm any threat he might appear to represent. As he climbed the creaking wooden stairs and stepped onto the safety of the covered porch, he began to breathe easier. He was stepping up to the door and raising his fist to knock when he noticed a symbol carved into the lintel above the door: something that looked like a "C" with two lines extending from either lip of the mouth. Hobo code, "The Owner is Out."

He trusted the code, but he knocked just to be

safe. No one answered, and he knocked again, which elicited not a single sign of stirring inside. He heaved a grateful sigh. The house was abandoned, it seemed. He shrugged out of his backpack, set it down against the wall beneath a tall narrow window next to the door, and walked to the edge of the porch. Looking out at the trees surrounding the meadow, he saw no opening by which to access the house. No way to just drive up to it. There was a narrow notch in the trees that marked the foot trail—the remnants of the gravel road—he'd arrived on, but no other obvious entry point. If ever there had been a road to this place, it had been overgrown by the forest long ago. The house had to be long abandoned.

But how could an abandoned house be in such fine shape considering its age?

Now that he'd determined that it was probably abandoned, the gloom and murk of the storm caused the house to take on an air of deep foreboding. But at that moment, he was too tired and wet to care.

A rickety wooden rocking chair at the other end of the porch caught his attention. It beckoned his weary muscles, and he sat down in it with great care, lest its wood be rotted and collapse beneath him. But it held, and he settled into it, sighing with relief as his stressed muscles relaxed. He would try the door later, after he'd been here a suitable time to allow anyone to protest his presence on the premises.

He fell instantly asleep.

The Mansion

When he awoke, he assumed that he had slept for several hours. He had no watch; when he had embarked upon his cross-country trek, he had resolved to be neither bound by time nor to march to the tick of the clock. So he had left his watch behind. But the moon, nearly three-quarters full, was flying high behind ragged clouds, and the storm had calmed into a quiet drizzle. His instincts told him it was near midnight, so midnight it was, as far as he was concerned. His clothes were still damp from his time in the downpour, but there was little he could do about it.

For several long moments, he sat staring at the runoff from the porch roof that shimmered a few feet in front of him, entranced by the constantly shifting rents in the liquid curtain.

Eventually he looked over at his backpack to make sure it was still safe. It was, but there were slivers of glass scattered on the porch around it. The tall narrow window beneath which he had placed the pack was broken; shards of glass stuck up from the frame like serrated teeth, making the darkness inside the house resemble the interior of the mouth of a predator. He hadn't noticed the broken glass when he had arrived. But he doubted he could have slept through the sound of shattering glass, even with the cover of the storm's thunder, so the window must have already been broken and he had simply been too tired and drenched to notice. He hadn't noticed a lot of things.

For instance, as his eyes swept across the front yard, he saw a high wall made of river stones that shone wetly in the moonlight and enclosed a wild, overgrown garden. The enclosure was accessed by an ornate stone archway in the wall facing the house. Within the archway, a rusty iron gate hung halfway off its hinges.

He also had not noticed the large pond to his right at the side of the house. Its calm water reflected the face of the nearly-full moon, obscured here and there by lily pads that floated serenely on the surface.

He looked away from the pond and surveyed the rest of the meadow. Its tall grass was plastered to the ground by the rains. Then, abruptly, his eyes snapped back to the pond.

Its surface was calm.

Strange and impossible, since a soft but steady rain was falling. No trees sheltered the pond, so its surface should have been pocked with spreading ripples from impacting raindrops.

Shrugging his shoulders, he turned his attention back to the porch. He had a trail bar tucked away in his backpack that would take the edge off the hunger gnawing at his gut. He stood and stretched, rubbing the kinks from his lower back. A day on the road followed by half a night in a rickety rocking chair was the perfect precursor for a chiropractic visit.

Stretch finished, he trudged to the backpack. He was just bending down and reaching for the pack when he noticed that the front door was ajar.

He straightened, abandoning the food bar as a shiver, born not of the chilly midnight air, raced up his spine—the door had most definitely not been standing open moments earlier, nor had it been upon his arrival, when he had knocked on a firmly closed door. His earlier knock might have loosened the door, priming it to swing open at the slightest breeze, but he doubted it.

He faced the narrow black line of the partially open door and fought to calm his racing heart. He felt a numinous presence in the air, an eldritch energy that raised his hackles; he had the sense of cold, musty air wafting from an ancient tomb.

Deliberately, he laughed out loud. He smiled and told himself he was being silly. He laughed again. And the chills racing up and down his spine died out, dispelled by his forced humor; the supernatural crackle of the air dissipated. If whatever spirits haunted these premises were inviting him inside, who was he to refuse? What did he care if death itself awaited him inside? He'd embarked upon this journey because he'd lost the will to live, but didn't have the courage to kill himself. So if there was an obliging spirit inside...

Boldly, he stepped forward and pushed the door all the way open. At least now he wouldn't have to force his way inside.

He turned from the door, intending to retrieve his backpack, and his eyes happened to fall upon the trees at the edge of the meadow.

A shape stood there, peering out at him from the trees, indistinct with distance and the intervening rain, but seemingly a woman, looking bedraggled and soggy as rainwater sluiced down her body, her flesh and clothing mostly gray in the moonlight. He nearly leapt out of his skin at the sight of her. And then a flash of lightning lit the night and momentarily blinded him, accompanied almost simultaneously by a deafening crack of thunder. When his eyes cleared, the apparition was gone; nothing but trees out there in the rain and the night, leaving him to wonder if he had imagined the woman.

He laughed again to dampen his fear. He retrieved his backpack, slung it over his shoulder, and stepped through the door into the darkness of the old house. His hand sought and found a light switch near the door, but when he flicked it, no lights flared. A second switch produced the same null result, and he gave up, assuming that the house had no active electrical supply. More evidence that the house had either been abandoned or perhaps winterized by an owner who intended to be absent for a long period.

He reached into his backpack and pulled forth a flashlight. He thumbed it on. The beam stabbed out across a spacious entrance hall, glinting dully off dust-covered bronze statues lining the wall to the left. Swiveling the light across the room to the wall opposite the door, the light reflected back at him from a large mirror. Holding up his left hand against the blinding glare, he saw his reflection standing silhouetted in the doorway, light emanating from the flashlight in his right hand. Dust and grime caked the surface of the mirror, so that he looked at himself as through a filmy curtain. Shining the light upward, a chandelier shattered the beam into a million facets, casting bright dancing circles of light onto the walls and floor.

He stepped forward, his feet shuffling through a layer of leaves and other detritus from outside that had apparently been blown inside through the broken window to the left of the door.

There were doorways in each of the walls, before him and to each side. Just beyond the doorways left and right were the dual wings of a grand staircase, which rose to a landing that ran the upper length of the rear wall of the hall, above the mirror.

"Hello!" he shouted. "I'm inside the house. I don't mean any harm. Just speak up, and I'll leave!"

He waited, but the house was silent, the utterly dead sort of silence that can only come from an empty house.

He stepped to his left and passed through the doorway into the room beyond. Shelves lined the walls from ceiling to floor, and all the shelves were sagging beneath the weight of books that looked to be as ancient as the house itself. Thick layers of dust coated the shelves and the books, and cobwebs were strung in the corners. The room—the library—had the musty smell of moldy parchment. Each step deeper into the room sent plumes of dust billowing into the air, freeing the accumulation of what seemed a hundred years from the huge rug that spanned nearly the whole of the library.

The ancient dust caught in his throat and tickled his nose, and he sneezed.

He dropped his backpack and sank down into a plush chair at the side of the room, unleashing more dust to assault his nose, and he went into a fit of coughing and sneezing.

When it had passed, he slouched gracelessly in the

chair, relaxing, and listened to the sound of the soft rain hitting the lone window behind him. On a small table beside the chair, three ancient tomes were opened and stacked one atop the other. He didn't bother checking the titles; plenty of time for that later.

Instead, his attention was caught by a portrait hanging on the opposite wall, next to the door through which he had entered. From within the confines of a gilded, ornate frame, a beautiful Victorian woman stared out at him, spotlighted by the beam of his flashlight like some celebrity of yesteryear.

The Painting

She was leaning on the railing of a staircase, indeed the same staircase that climbed to the front porch of this very house. She struck a pose that was at once both demure and yet erotically charged. She wore a white dress trimmed in lace at the hem and cuffs and high-buttoned collar, with a lacy belt cinching a too-narrow waist that hinted at the presence of a corset. A fan dangled from her right hand, while her left elbow rested on the staircase railing, with the palm of her left hand cradling her chin. Her shy, half-lidded gaze was, ironically, frank and perhaps a bit wanton. The pinky-finger of her left hand, unlike her other delicate fingers, which were tucked beneath her chin, extended up to the edge of her pouting, crimson lips in a way that was vaguely lascivious. Fiery red hair tumbled out beneath a black bonnet, contrasting starkly with the alabaster skin of her beautiful face.

The background of the painting was a montage of strange images, arrayed in a circle behind the woman. There were wet, stony steps descending into a dark tunnel with dripping stone walls. There was a mysteriously calm pond which he recognized as the one which lay at the side of this very house. There was the archway of the walled garden at the front of the house. There was a small trap door in the ceiling of some vague room. He could not fathom the reason for the inclusion of the images in the montage, and at that moment, he didn't care. He was too entranced with the beautiful woman, too taken by the deep longing that seemed to emanate from her gaze.

He wondered who she had been. A previous mistress of the house, perhaps the last owner? Could this house really have been abandoned that long, since the Victorian era? Surely not.

He took a deep breath. He thought about continuing his exploration of the house. But that could wait. It had been a while since he had been in anyone's company and he was lonely, so he remained sitting in the chair, meeting the woman's longing gaze. An echoing yearn swelled in his heart, a deep regret that they were separated by the veil of years. He felt as if that frank gaze regarded him as a long-awaited visitor who had, to her vexation, arrived too late. He longed to hold her, to cross the room and take that delicate, delicious woman into his arms and just hold her. But it was too late.

He sat in the chair well into the small hours of the morning, staring across at the painting and across an unbridgeable gap of time and space. He could not shake the sensation that she was somehow studying him as intensely as he studied her. As if she were assessing him, measuring him. He gazed at the painting nearly unblinkingly until sleep finally claimed him.

When he awoke, the light of late morning was shining in through the half-open drapes behind him. Sometime after he had fallen asleep, his flashlight had dropped from his relaxed hand. It now lay on the floor. He retrieved it, and discovered that the batteries had been depleted. Since the batteries were his last, he would have to find an alternate source of light if he intended to stay another night.

He put the flashlight down on the small table beside him. Idly, he now looked at the titles of the books lying open thereupon.

The first, at the bottom of the stack, was an early edition, perhaps a first, of *The Wonderful Wizard of Oz*. No doubt he could sell it for a hefty sum if he were to place it in his backpack and take it to the nearest city.

The second tome was a very early edition of *Alice's Adventures in Wonderland*. Also sure to fetch a good price if he were to abscond with it.

The third was a hardcover edition of Stephen King's *The Gunslinger*. The presence of the modern-day book seemed to belie his tentative assessment that the mansion had been abandoned for a long time. He supposed if he took the King book, he might be able to sell it for a penny or two through an online marketplace, rendering the volume pretty much useless to him.

But of course he would take none of the books: he was no thief.

Finally he let his eyes wander back to the portrait next to the door and drank in the lovely image.

Strange. He felt he had stared at the portrait long enough during the night to have memorized every line of the woman's beautiful face. But a small detail seemed to have escaped him: One corner of her delicious pouting mouth was curved upward in a slight smile.

He stood and crossed the room to stand before the aged painting. He reached out and traced the line of her mouth with his right index finger. Then he moved upward to the red hair spilling out from beneath her bonnet, made a motion as if he were brushing the hair from her eyes, as a lover might. He smiled at her, lifted his finger and pressed it to his lips.

He looked downward, a sinuous line of faded gold paint catching his eye. There were two lines of writing along the bottom edge of the portrait, underscored by the hard edge of the wooden frame. Written in an elegant cursive script, the faded lines read,

> *Scattered by the wind that blows across four worlds,*
> *She longs to come back home, this poor, ensorcelled girl.*

Strange that he had missed this detail as well during last night's long scrutiny of the portrait. Strange words as well, hinting at some sort of fantastic element to the woman in the portrait. Or were the words merely a line from some unknown-to-him old poem favored by the woman?

Reluctantly, he tore his gaze away from the portrait. He was hungry, both for food and to explore the rest of the mansion.

He went to his backpack and rooted around for a food bar. He noted with some concern that only three of the bars remained. He had intended to be in the next town along the road by now, where he could resupply. An extended stay in the back-country hadn't been on his current agenda. So if he was to stay in this old mansion for any length of time, food would be a priority.

He stood, unwrapped the food bar, and slowly ate as he wandered back to the entrance hall to begin his explorations.

The door directly across the entrance hall from the library led to a large dining room. A long rectangular table filled most of the room. Elegant, stately chairs lined both of the long sides of the table, while either end, where the master and the mistress of the mansion would have customarily sat, was furnished with an immense, throne-like chair.

The daylight that oozed in from around the edges of the drawn curtains of the tall windows along the wall to the right cast the room in a dusky half-twilight. Dust motes hung thick in the air, further suffusing the light. That, combined with the musty, stale odor that hung in the air, made the dining room seem oppressively heavy with the weight of long years.

Beyond the dining room he found an industrial sized kitchen, fit for a castle. The kitchen cupboards were bare, lacking any cook- or silver-ware. He did, however, find a pantry just off the kitchen, which was stocked with shelf after shelf of canned goods, home-made preserves, military MREs, and great big plastic containers of freeze-dried foods. It appeared that someone had been stockpiling to survive the aftermath of an apocalypse, with types of foods that were made to last for decades.

The food had certainly outlived the soldier who had apparently been the one stocking the shelves with doomsday meals, for he lay on the floor of the pantry, right where he had died, a collection of bones dressed in green and brown Army camouflage khakis. Of course, it was an assumption that the soldier had been a *he*; it was also an assumption that the pile of bones had been a soldier. The eye sockets of the dead soldier's skull stared up at him as he peered into the pantry, as if wondering who was raiding the place.

He took one quick look at the skeleton, then grabbed an armful of the MREs from a shelf and ducked back out of the pantry. At least his food shortage was now solved. The few packs he had grabbed should keep him from having to face the skeleton of the soldier again for several days, at least. He didn't know if he would be here that long, but for the first time in a long time, he wasn't feeling too eager to hit the road again. He was beginning to feel anchored to this place, anchored by the woman in the painting.

Who had the soldier been? Her lover, perhaps? He felt a stab of jealousy. But that didn't make sense. The soldier's uniform had looked relatively modern, probably not more than half a century out of date. That placed him too late to have crossed paths with the Victorian-era woman in the painting. Who, then? Perhaps another wanderer who had become smitten with the painting, and whiled away his hours in this mansion until he'd wasted away? That wasn't a very attractive thought.

He brought the MREs back into the dining room and set them onto the table for his later convenience. Then he crossed back into the entrance hall and passed through the door opposite the front door.

Beyond was a long hallway that ran toward the back of the mansion. Numerous doors opened off it.

Through the first door to the right, he found a grand saloon, a spacious room with two large fireplaces and several plush sofas, as well as numerous chairs grouped into small conversational areas. There was an antique brass spittoon in one corner, and a glass-doored hutch with a collection of delicate chinaware on display within. The carpet of the saloon was a regal purple.

In one corner of the saloon was a small door with peeling white paint and a brass doorknob worn smooth from long use. He opened the door to reveal a large, empty closet. There was nothing, no shelves, no items one might typically find in a closet, no hangars— nothing. The lone item of interest in the closet was the small trap door in the center of the ceiling. A small cord dangled from the edge of the door, so that one might pull the door down. But the end of the cord was beyond his reach, and would require the aid of a step stool or some such tool. He didn't bother to fetch one. He just filed the trap door away in his mind as an item for possible future investigation.

Closing the closet door, he left the saloon.

Over the next several hours, he explored the rest of the mansion. On the ground floor, he found a smoking room, a drawing room, a second library, a bathroom with turn-of-the-century-before-last plumbing and fixtures, and a waiting room. Upstairs, he found half a dozen bedrooms, a second, larger bathroom, and a laundry room. He also found a flight of stairs that led to a dark, dusty attic cluttered with boxes, old furniture, and several huge spiderwebs that caused him to turn tail and flee back downstairs. He hated spiders.

All the rooms of the mansion had furniture suited to the function of the particular room: beds, sofas, bookcases, dressers, desks. Pretty mundane furniture that was remarkable only for its antique nature.

Near noon, he stepped back out onto the front

porch. The storm of the previous night had departed, leaving sunshine in the sky and rapidly diminishing puddles in the grassy meadow surrounding the house. The tall, unmown grass was regaining its rigidity and springing back up as it dried out.

He leaned against the railing of the porch, surveying the meadow in the daylight. Since he had only seen it previously in the pitch black of a storm-tossed night, he was now seeing it as if for the first time. He looked at the decaying, six-foot high stone wall that enclosed the overgrown garden (of course, from his current position on the porch, he couldn't tell if it actually was overgrown; he would need to pass through the wrought-iron arch and into the enclosure to make that determination; but from the profuse vegetation poking above the top of the wall, he stuck by his initial assessment). He looked again at the stagnant pond at the side of the house, wondering anew at its utterly placid surface, even in the face of the rather strong breeze currently wafting through the area.

He looked too at the distant line of trees, unbroken all the way around the meadow, with no way for automobiles to drive up to the house. The only way to access the meadow was by the meager trail he had followed in the night, the trail that had started off as a gravel road branching from the county road beyond the woods. The trail head was visible as a small opening in the dark line of trees, almost directly in front of him.

It was an utterly peaceful place. The sight of such beauty, such isolation, and the tranquility of it, made him feel more calm and content than he'd felt in many months. He could easily see himself remaining here for a few days, weeks, maybe a month or more. Maybe longer, he thought, as the face of the woman in the picture flashed across the canvas of his mind.

As soon as her lovely face graced his mind, he realized that he was presently leaning upon the very railing on which she had leaned so long ago, in posing for the painted portrait. Had he unconsciously, instinctively chosen to lean against it? If so, it only proved how indelibly she had been pressed into his mind, like a seal pressed into wax.

A thrill raced through him. To think that she had once stood here, almost in this very spot, for an unknown period of time, patiently holding a pose as some unknown artist captured her loveliness in paint, preserving it for the ages! Preserving it for him.

A thought occurred to him: what if the woman in the painting wasn't real? What if she was merely the product of the painter's imagination? What if the painter was actually the soldier whose bones even now moldered in the kitchen pantry? What if he weren't a soldier at all, but merely some fanatical doomsday prepper who had chosen this remote location to wait out the inevitable apocalypse? What did that then make the woman in the painting? The defecation of a lunatic mind?

No.

He couldn't bring himself to believe that she wasn't real. A human mind couldn't imagine such loveliness into existence. Such loveliness could only be captured, not created.

He became aware of a piece of paper flapping on a porch post a few feet from him. The paper was tacked into the wood of the post. The ambient breeze stirred the paper, making it seem as if the paper were flapping for his attention.

He stepped over to the post and put out a hand, smoothing the paper. There was something written on it. A message, crafted in an elegant, old-fashioned calligraphy: "Find the Key of the Ancients." Just a short, meaningless message.

He removed the paper from the tack, and reread the message several times. What was the Key of the Ancients?

He was certain the paper hadn't been here when he'd arrived. The strong winds of the storm would surely have blown it away, and if not, then the driving rain would have smeared the ink-written message into illegibility.

The implications of the paper note sent an icy chill up his spine. He wasn't alone! Someone had recently left the note for him to find.

The Stairs

He looked up and around in alarm. Almost immediately, he caught sight of a person standing near the distant trail head, looking at him from the edge of the woods. It was the same woman he thought he'd imagined seeing the previous night, during the waning hours of the storm. She wore the same drab gray clothing, still looking wet and bedraggled despite the absence of the storm and the warmth of the sun. A nimbus of gray fog seemed to hang about her face, so that her face was vague, her features fuzzy, indistinct. It almost seemed as if she *had* no features. But surely that was just a trick of the distance.

There was something unnerving about her, some sort of numinous, eldritch energy emanating from her, that raised the hackles on the back of his neck. He couldn't see her eyes, but he could feel them upon him, unblinking.

He swallowed a lump in his throat. "Hello!" he called across to her. "I hope I'm not intruding. I mean, I don't mean to. My name's Kurt."

She gave no response, no indication that she heard or understood him.

Kurt waved the paper note. "Did you leave this note for me? What does it mean?"

Still no response.

He tucked the note into the pocket of his jeans,

then took a slow step forward, down the porch stairs. When his foot touched the cobble-stoned walkway overgrown with grass, and he'd started across the meadow toward her, she turned and bolted into the woods like a frightened deer.

He stopped, peering for long moments at the spot where she had been, but she didn't reappear.

He crossed the meadow, his feet squishing in the mud, the dewy grass quickly soaking his pant-legs. When he reached the spot where she'd been, the ground was muddy, but substantial enough that footprints should have been retained.

There were none.

"It's okay!" he shouted into the woods. "I won't hurt you! Do you live in the mansion? I think I'll stay for a few days. If you want me to leave, just tell me, and I'll go."

He waited a long time for a response, or for her to show herself again, but he was met only with the sounds of nature: the chirping of birds, the rush of wind through the trees, the low chirruping of crickets.

He turned and retraced his steps to the house.

Back in the dining room, Kurt tore open one of the MREs. By some clever trick of chemical engineering, they heated themselves as soon as he tore along the perforated line, so he wouldn't need an oven or a camp stove to make them edible. He ate a quiet meal at the dining room table, listening to the sounds of the house settling around him as he chewed.

When he was through, he went back out onto the patio, hoping the strange woman might have gotten over her fright and returned. He searched the distant boundary of trees where he had last seen her, but she wasn't there.

Movement at the corner of his vision caught his attention. He turned to his left, and thought to glimpse someone just disappearing around the far corner of the house.

"Wait!" he called out. He bounded down the patio steps in pursuit. Rounding the corner of the house, he found...

...no one.

He cast his gaze about wildly, searching. There was nowhere anyone could have gotten to so quickly, nowhere to hide from him. Maybe he'd imagined the movement?

He looked at the ground. The dewy grass seemed slightly disturbed, possibly by someone's passage. But it was such a slight disturbance, it might have been merely his mind playing tricks, seeing what it wanted to see.

If anyone had come this way, it was conceivable that they might have managed to round the far corner of the house before he'd rounded the corner behind him. But the person would had to have been moving very fast. The only other possible refuge was a pair of slanted doors that angled off the house midway between the corners—probably the entrance to a cellar. But the doors were closed. In the split-seconds he'd hesitated before pursuing, the person definitely could not have opened the doors, fled inside, and closed the doors.

He stood there at the side of the house for several long moments, listening. Then: "Hello?" he called out.

He heard nothing but the sighing of the wind.

Concluding that he hadn't really seen anything

from the corner of his eye, he stepped toward the cellar doors, curious. They were wooden, sagging inward with age. The hinges were rusty and brittle; rusty handles graced the center of each door; the handle on the left door swung on one screw, the other screw having decayed and broken off in years long past.

He reached down, grasped the bottom edge of the left-hand door, and heaved upward. With a loud groaning creak of protest, the door swung up. Just beyond the apex of its swing, he let go, and the door's own weight carried it back to the ground with a jarring crash.

A gaping black maw now opened into the ground. The afternoon light revealed a cobweb-strung throat slanting into the ground beneath the mansion. Stony, moss-covered steps disappeared down into the darkness. The unbroken cobwebs hanging across the maw spoke to the fact that no one had passed downward in quite some time.

The cellar entrance creeped him out. He imagined monsters slumbering beneath the house, in some sort of secret, forgotten laboratory, or perhaps the lair of a Victorian-era serial killer. And yet the entrance beckoned, like a newly discovered crypt calling out to the failed archeologist within him. Architect, archeologist, doctor, astronaut, movie star—he'd wanted to be all of those things, and many others, at various points in his life. That had always been part of his problem—never knowing what he really wanted to be. And so he sampled everything. Had he been born in some other age, he would have been romanticized as a Renaissance man. In this age, however, men like him were derided as restless and lazy, as dilettantes.

He looked into the dark maw, watching a spider climbing up a dangling strand of its web. He shivered in revulsion, and had second thoughts about venturing into the cellar.

He drew himself up. Spiders or no, he would brave the cellars depths. The house had been a part of *her*, and he wanted to discover all its secrets.

But he couldn't go stumbling blindly down in the darkness. He would need light. And thus he was confronted with the fact that his flashlight batteries were dead, and the house had no electricity. Regardless of whether or not he ventured into the cellar, he was going to have to solve his light problem before nightfall.

Then he remembered the antique-looking oil lamps he'd seen in the hallways of the house, and on various tables in the rooms of the house. He'd noticed them earlier on his exploration, but hadn't given them any thought at the time.

Surely they wouldn't have oil in them after all these years? Wouldn't oil have long since evaporated? Or if it hadn't, wouldn't it have been rendered inert by the long years? Then again, he really had no idea how long the house had actually been empty. The idea that the house hadn't been occupied since Victorian times was just an invention of his mind, a foolishly romantic little fantasy based only upon the painting of a beautiful Victorian woman in the library. Considered in the cold light of reality, it was really an idiotic idea. After all, the dead doomsday prepper in the pantry seemed to belie his fantasy.

He went back into the house and checked the first

oil lamp he could find, in the hallway near the saloon. The worn brass tank of the thing was nearly half full of oil. Kerosene. He took it down from its sconce, and retrieved a book of matches from his backpack, still in the library where he'd left it. He paused momentarily to stare at the painting, grinning at the woman, tracing her beautiful enigmatic smile with his eyes.

Then, returning to the side of the house and the cellar entrance, he removed the glass bulb from the lamp and, striking a match, lit the wick. Then he put the glass back on the lamp, sheltering the precious flame from the breeze.

He found an arm-length stick lying in the grass near the cellar entrance. He picked it up and, sweeping it before him, using it to swat the cob- and spider-webs from his path, he began his descent into the cellar.

As he took his first few steps, the light from the oil lamp flickered on the walls of the tunnel, walls made of stone bricks that were covered with moss and dripping with condensation. The tunnel descended steeply, more steeply than he'd expected. He'd also expected to reach a cellar, a cramped, earthy room beneath the house, after a few steps.

Instead, the lamplight merely revealed a long flight of stone stairs descending at a sharp angle, disappearing into the darkness at the edge of the lamp's range.

He paused on the sixth step down. A sense of deja-vu washed over him. He'd seen this sight before: stairs in a tunnel disappearing down into darkness. It took him a moment to realize where he'd seen this before, and when he did, a shiver raced up his spine:

this was one of the images in the montage in the painting. In *her* painting. What did it signify? What was so special about the cellar, or rather, these stairs (since by now he was beginning to think that the cellar was another construction of his imagination), that they should be included in the painting?

Prompted by the realization that he was stepping into an image from the paining, he remembered the trap door in the ceiling of the closet in the saloon: it too was featured in the painting. As was the stone-wall-enclosed garden, and the pond at the other side of the house.

What was the connection between the images of the montage? More importantly, what was their connection to the woman?

He was more intrigued than ever to see where the stairs went.

He stepped downward, clutching the ancient oil lamp in his left hand, the right hand trailing along the wall to steady himself. The stairs were very steep. After he'd gone down thirty steps, counting them out, he reached a short landing. The tunnel turned sharply right, and the oil lamp revealed another flight of stone steps descending into darkness.

He paused on the landing and examined the wall of bricks carefully, looking for signs of a hidden door, something to indicate an entrance to the cellar.

He found nothing.

He descended the second flight of stairs. The air grew noticeably cold and clammy, and reeked of earthy things like worms and wet clay and roots.

Thirty more steps brought him to a second landing. Another sharp turn to the right revealed a third flight of stairs descending steeply into darkness.

By his estimation he was now at least thirty feet below ground, with no sign of a cellar, and every indication that the stairs continued downward indefinitely.

He'd never heard of such a thing. Where could this stone staircase be leading? To what secret underground lair, to what forgotten underground grotto?

He put a foot forward to continue his descent.

And the light from the oil lamp was abruptly extinguished by an unearthly cold breeze that suddenly swept up from below, somehow managing to penetrate the glass of the lamp and douse the flame.

Pitch blackness enveloped him, and a primal fear welled up from the depths of his being. He dropped the oil lamp, and by the time it struck the ground, the glass shattering, he was already back up on the first landing and scrambling back up the first flight of stairs toward the square of daylight that beckoned so high above.

He practically exploded from the cellar entrance, and as he stood in the grass with the afternoon sun beating down on him, trying to calm his racing heart, he was amazed that he'd made it out so quickly without cracking his head open as he'd stumbled up the slick mossy stairs in the darkness.

When he'd calmed down, he looked back at the cellar entrance. He'd go back, eventually. But not yet. She didn't want him going down there. Not yet.

He bent over and grabbed the cellar door, swinging it back up and then down, closing the entrance for the time being. Trapping the foul and unholy things that were, in his imagination, slowly rising up those bottomless stairs.

What to do now?

He trudged around to the front of the house. At the foot of the stairs, he paused to scan the distant tree line. Still no sign of the mysterious woman. He began to doubt that he'd ever really seen her at all.

The Key of the Ancients

Kurt climbed the porch stairs, entered the mansion and went into the library. He faced the painting, putting his hands behind his back and assuming a stance from which to make a dispassionate study of the thing. Seeking clues. The woman stared back, the corners of her mouth perked up in that perpetual smirk.

He looked at the montage around her. The pond... The walled garden... The trap door in the ceiling... The stairs into the earth...

His eyes caught on the fan that dangled from the woman's right hand. The line of it seemed to form a sort of arrow, pointing...

...pointing to a decorative shrub at the foot of the stairs, a rose bush. He looked closely at the bush. Among an intricate network of thorny branches and flowering red buds, the artist had painted a key lying on the shadowy ground. The key was barely visible unless one looked closely. Almost, it seemed an optical illusion, a trick of the bush's shadows and branches. It was an old-fashioned skeleton key, with a thick golden shank and a single tooth set with diamonds. The bow was in the shape of a heart.

He pulled the piece of paper from his pocket and reread the note: "Find the Key of the Ancients."

He looked at the woman. "Is that the Key of the

Ancients?" he asked her, pointing at the key half-hidden in the bush.

She didn't answer.

He put the note back in his pocket, and went out onto the porch. He stood at the top of the stairs, looking down to the foot, where the bush was depicted in the painting. There was no bush there now. Either the bush had never really existed, and was merely an embellishment by the artist, or it had died long ago. He imagined the latter

He descended the steps and, once on the ground, dropped to his knees. Where the bush had once grown, he rooted through the overgrown grass with his hands, searching by touch. He felt nothing save the dew and the willowy blades.

He dug into the soft, wet dirt, his fingers burrowing like worms into the earth. And they encountered something. Something cold and hard, narrow. The shank of a key! He grasped the metal cylinder and pulled, tugging it free from the ground in a shower of dirt.

It was just as it had been depicted in the painting: an old-fashioned skeleton key. But, unlike the painting, the gold of this key was tarnished and dull, the diamonds in the single tooth were caked with dirt. And most of the bow had been broken off, so that only a single short section of the heart shape remained, such a small section that, had he not already known it was supposed to be part of a heart, it would not have been obvious.

He sat back on his haunches, clutching the cold metal in his hands. "Okay, I've got it!" he shouted. "Now what?" He didn't know who he expected to answer. The mysterious gray woman? The woman in the painting?

But he received no answer, and he let out a pent-up breath. He chuckled. "Fool," he chided himself.

He put the Key in his breast pocket, and fastened the button. Even through the thick fabric of his shirt, the Key was cold and heavy. The broken heart of the bow rested right above his own heart.

He stood.

A key, he thought. I've got a key. Okay. Keys unlock things. Doors, usually. Might there be a locked door somewhere in the house that the Key would open?

Doors. Doors. He thought back over his recent tour of the house. Had he noted any locked doors? And then he recalled the only door that made any sense.

The trap door in the closet ceiling! The door featured in the painting's montage.

The Closet

Kurt raced into the house and veered right, into the dining room. He took hold of one of the elegant chairs arrayed along the dining table, and dragged the heavy thing into the saloon. Opening the closet door, he dragged the chair to the center of the cramped closet. For a long moment, he stood with hands on hips and looked up at the trap door in the ceiling. It was square, of course, about three feet to a side. It fit so perfectly into the ceiling that the seams of the door were only visible as a hairline gap. The thing that really made the door stand out from the ceiling was its color. Unlike the closet ceiling, which was painted egg-shell white that had stained toward the yellow over the years, the door was a garish red. Red, the color of blood, of hearts. And the Key of the Ancients in the painting had a heart-shaped bow. It couldn't be a coincidence.

And yes, there it was, next to where the fraying rope dangled from one edge of the door: a large keyhole, most likely a perfect fit for the shank of the Key of the Ancients.

He climbed onto the chair he'd brought from the dining room. Then he reached into his breast pocket and pulled out the Key. Reaching upward, slowly and carefully to maintain his balance, he raised the Key toward the keyhole in the trap door. It slid inside, a perfect fit. He twisted, and as he did so, he had the strange sensation that he had just unlocked a turning point in his life. A bolt inside the trap door slid aside and clicked, and then a dead, ominous silence seemed to fall over the entire house. The distant creaking of the house as it settled went away, as did the faint sound of the wind whistling through cracks and vents. All sound vanished, so that all he could hear was the beating of his own heart.

He took a deep breath, then took hold of the frayed dangling rope and pulled it downward.

The trap door swiveled down on creaking hinges until it hung perpendicular to the ceiling, revealing a square shaft that climbed upward into darkness. There were rusted iron rungs on one wall of the shaft, forming a ladder to allow ascent upward.

The walls of the shaft itself, above the thin layer of drywall and wood paneling that formed the ceiling of the closet, were made of red brick. The scent of moldy bricks wafted down to his upturned nostrils, and ancient dust drifted gently down upon his face.

He coughed, and blinked as his eyes began to burn in the dusty rain, which was rapidly lessening. He imagined that the dust was the remnants of generations of mouse poop, now aerosolized and carrying the spores of ancient diseases into his eyes and nose.

He pulled the Key of the Ancients from the keyhole, and tucked it safely back into his breast pocket.

Then he took hold of the bottom rung. The iron was cold and rough against his curled fingers. He fought to pull himself up into the shaft, his legs swinging free of the chair as his arms alone bore the weight of his body, pulling him upward until he was far enough inside that his feet were able to find purchase on the rungs and ease the burden. From then on it would be as simple as climbing an ordinary ladder. He paused to catch his breath, looking upward into the darkness. He would have delayed his climb long enough to retrieve an oil lamp such as the one he'd earlier lost on his descent down the stairs. But he figured the shaft only went up to a second floor room, perhaps out onto the roof, so he doubted he would need the lamp, expecting to find light peeking through the cracks of the far end of the shaft, providing ample light.

So he began climbing upward. The shaft was cramped, barely large enough to allow him to move his limbs. He felt cobwebs brushing against his face as he climbed through the darkness, and began to wish that he'd taken the time to fetch a lamp after all. He did so hate spiders!

But he wouldn't allow his fears to override his excitement. Like the stairs leading into the ground, this shaft was some sort of connection to *her*, and he was determined to learn the nature of the connection.

After a couple of minutes of climbing, he felt sure he must have ascended at least three times his own height: more than enough to have reached the second floor of the mansion. He stopped and clung to the rungs. By now his eyes had adjusted to the darkness of the shaft, and there was still enough daylight filtering up from the closet, so that he was just able to make out the bricks and the rungs. But that was *all* he could make out. He saw no evidence of egress onto the second floor, neither a blatant door nor a secret one. He felt the bricks all around him, just to be sure, and his fingers confirmed the assessment of his eyes: there was no apparent entrance to the second floor.

He craned his neck upward to check out the ceiling. Astonishingly, there *was* no ceiling. The shaft continued upward. He thought he could discern a faint light filtering down from somewhere high above. An exit onto the roof, perhaps?

He resumed his climb. By the time he had ascended three or four more times his own height, he figured he should at least be level with the attic, if not the roof. Yet he still hadn't reached the source of the light he'd thought he'd seen at his first stop.

He paused in his climb and looked upward. The shaft continued, its square lines converging to a vanishing point high above. It was definitely lighter up there. But how could the shaft possibly go so high? By his estimation, the vanishing point was...he had no idea how high up it was. But the vanishing point was so distant that the shaft most definitely would have to extend well beyond the roof of the mansion. It would even have to extend past both the central clock tower and the western spire-topped tower.

It was flat impossible.

He looked at the walls around him, searching for signs of a door or hatch to the attic or the inside of one of the towers. A seam of light, perhaps, or a cool draft against his skin. But he found nothing.

And so he continued climbing.

He counted off body lengths each time he'd climbed his own height.

One.

Two.

Three.

Four.

Five...

...Fifteen.

He paused. The muscles of his arms and legs were burning with strain. His fingers felt arthritic from clamping so tightly around the iron rungs. As he clung to the side of the shaft, he calculated how high up he was. He was six feet tall to the inch. Six feet times fifteen: ninety feet. He was ninety feet up the shaft, by rough estimation. Perhaps a bit more, perhaps a bit less.

It was impossible! The mansion had definitely not reared ninety feet above the meadow. And he hadn't seen a vertical shaft of brick extending above the house like some extraordinarily high chimney. How could he possibly have climbed so high?

He looked upward. He could now see a definite square of light high above, where the ceiling of the shaft would be. But it was way up there, maybe half again as high as he'd already climbed.

He looked down. The square of light where the entrance to the closet would be was so distant it was no longer even visible. There was nothing but darkness below his feet.

His muscles protested as he resumed climbing.

Seven body lengths later, he was just approaching the square of light. Sky was visible, a gray sky with roiling gray clouds. Warm, humid air that smelled of impending rain drifted down into the shaft and felt clammy against his skin. That was strange, since he'd been outside not more than an hour earlier, and there hadn't been a cloud in the sky, just sunshine and the deep blue sky of a summer afternoon.

He reached the lip of the shaft and gripped it, pulling himself carefully up and out. Out onto a plain of barren, glassy black rock.

Eye in the Sky

Kurt knelt near the edge of the square opening in the ground out of which he had climbed, looking about in utter disbelief.

The plain of black rock extended from gray horizon to gray horizon, broken by occasional outcroppings of rock, like jagged hills. There was no grass or other vegetation, and no sign of animal life. No birds flew in the sky. There was just an endless expanse of black, rocky ground, and a leaden gray sky with gray clouds that roiled restlessly like smoke from a chimney.

This was impossible! His mind protested at the sight. He had climbed into a shaft in the closet of a mansion at the center of a meadow. He'd climbed at least one hundred and forty feet above that meadow, only to climb out of the ground onto this barren plain. He had climbed into the sky and emerged from the ground.

Impossible! The stairs that led ever downward beneath the house had seemed strange and unlikely, but this...this was flat impossible! Not only that, it was disorienting. Was the mansion still somewhere beneath him, somewhere through the ground? He couldn't shake the feeling that he was somehow standing on top of the sky above the mansion, and that was flatly impossible.

He stood and stumbled forward, gaping at the world around him. He came abreast of one of the rocky outcroppings, a hill of jagged rock. Just beyond it, he found a gnarly oak tree that had been hidden from view by the hill as he'd knelt beside the shaft. On the bole of the oak tree was carved a circle with an arrow pointing to the right: hobo code for "This way."

He looked at the tree, dumbfounded, for it was the same tree he had seen the previous night when he'd been caught out in the storm. The same tree that had led him to the mansion. Yet how could it possibly be the same tree? This couldn't even be the same world, for God's sake! Surely he had entered some nightmare corner of his own mind. Had he finally snapped, and climbed upward into his own hallucination?

If so, then surely it was best to go back the way he had come, to descend back down the shaft, back into sanity.

He stumbled away from the oak tree with its hobo code message, and retreated back around the hill of black rock.

But the square opening in the ground was gone. He threw himself to the ground and scoured the rock in a panic. He wasn't mistaken; the opening had been right here! He hadn't gone far enough to have gotten lost. It had been right here, at this precise spot!

He slapped at the glassy black rock, the solid black rock where the opening to the shaft should have been. He slapped at the ground as if that would make the shaft opening reappear. He slapped so hard his palms stung, but the rock was unyielding. This was no door in disguise, camouflaging the shaft entrance. No, this was solid rock, as solid as if the shaft had never been here at all.

Still kneeling, he huddled in on himself and whimpered. He began to tremble, as the breeze was chill, raising gooseflesh on his bare forearms.

He looked around the bleak gray world. Where could he go, what could he do? What was this place?

Somewhere off to his left, a woman's scream ripped through the air, offering a course of action. He leapt to his feet. He moved forward a few uncertain feet. The scream came again, allowing him to orient on it: behind one of the rocky outcroppings about a quarter of a mile to his left.

He ran. The black rock of the ground was as slick as the glass it resembled. His feet slipped constantly and threatened to send him skidding down onto his face. But he adjusted, and was able to run at a reasonable clip without breaking any limbs or bones.

For a brief instant as he ran, the roiling clouds above him parted and he thought to glimpse an enormous eye peering down at him from the sky. Almost before his mind could even process the sight and register astonishment and fright, the clouds closed in to fill the brief gap, and he told himself he couldn't possibly have seen what he thought.

The scream came again, louder now that he was drawing near. He raced around the outcropping, now a large hill of tumbled glossy black rocks with jagged edges. Beyond, he found an altar of black obsidian, like the ground. Bound with rope by the wrists and ankles to two large iron spikes driven into either end of the altar was a girl who was perhaps in her mid-to-high teens. She was completely nude and spread-eagled, struggling against her bonds. Her luxuriant blond hair fell like a waterfall past her shoulders and over her budding breasts. Her skin was alabaster white and glowed with youthful vitality. And her face...He could think of no description that was more apt than *angelic*. Overall, she was so radiantly pure he almost couldn't bear to look at her. Her light seared into the darkest places of his soul, burning him. Her big blue eyes seemed the very epitome of innocence as she turned them upon him and pleaded, "Help me!"

He cast a hasty glance around the area, but saw no one else, no adults that might offer resistance if he tried to free her. He rushed forward, looming above her, and began undoing the knot in the rope binding one of her slender ankles. The rope was knotted around one ankle, then passed through a loop in the end of the iron spike nearest her feet, and continued on to knot around her other ankle.

The knot was tied expertly and tightly, and he struggled to tease it apart.

"Who did this to you?" he asked the girl as he worked. Out of respect for her nudity, he carefully avoided looking up at her, instead focusing on the knot.

"My tribe," she said. "Hurry, they've already seen me and will be coming soon!"

"Who? Your tribe?" He looked away from his work on the knot, wary. But he saw no one approaching, and so returned to the knot. He'd almost gotten it undone.

"No!" she whispered. "Them!" And she pointed. Not at the landscape around her, but up into the sky.

Reluctantly, he again took his gaze away from the knot and looked upward.

Enormous tentacles were reaching through the clouds, from the *other side* of the clouds. Reaching down toward him and the girl. They were gray and slick, perhaps from moisture in the clouds or from slime secreted from subcutaneous glands. There were a dozen of them, as thick as tree trunks, undulating and writhing like snakes as they descended slowly from the heavens.

"What the hell?" he hissed. And he remembered the eye he had seen. It hadn't been his imagination, and it had probably seen him as well. Some sort of monstrous creature living in the sky, above the clouds?

The girl screamed.

And he suddenly realized: she was a sacrifice, like Andromeda staked out for the Kraken.

His fingers scrabbled madly against her ankle, twisting and tugging at the knot. Finally it came loose, and she kicked her ankle free. He didn't bother with the other ankle, and neither did she. There wasn't time. They left the rope to trail free from her other ankle while both of them turned their attention to her wrists. She sat up and held her wrists out for him as he knelt beside her and tugged furiously at the knot.

"Hurry!" she whimpered, peering up at the sky with wide eyes. "They're almost here!"

He didn't pause to look; the sight would only have distracted him.

With a final tug, the knot and the rope dropped away from her wrist, and they were up and running across the smooth rock. He pushed the girl ahead of him, helping her along and shielding her as best he could.

Some sort of higher sense, instinct perhaps, made

him peer backward as he ran. One of the huge tentacles undulated mere inches away from his head. The tip of it was a huge phallus, a huge, erect, quite human phallus. The rest of the tentacle curved away up into the sky. There were half a dozen more immediately behind and to either side.

He increased his speed and grabbed hold of the girl, tackling her as gently as he could, bearing her to the ground. There was no other choice; the tentacles would have them otherwise. He had no weapons, and no idea where he might find shelter.

The girl squealed as they toppled together, then huffed as she hit the ground and he came down on top of her, knocking the wind out of her.

The tentacles went racing past where they would have been if they'd kept on. Then the things stopped and undulated in place, quivering, as though confused.

He looked up, watching them, wondering why they weren't still reaching for him. Or for the girl.

The clouds above parted, and that enormous eye peered down, scanning back and forth aimlessly, as though searching. That eerie gaze passed right over him several times, not seeming to see him.

It was as if he were invisible to whatever beast was concealed beyond the clouds. And as he was covering the girl with his body, she too was invisible to it. She struggled beneath him, not to get away, but to squirm to a more comfortable position so she could draw breath.

He levered himself upward slightly on his knees and hands, easing his weight. It was a familiar action, though one he hadn't had to perform in more years than he cared to admit. "Stay under me," he whispered. "I don't think it can see me. Maybe because I don't belong here. I don't know what else it could be."

The tentacles hadn't been chasing both of them; they'd had been chasing her alone. The tentacles—the eye in the sky—probably hadn't even been aware of his presence.

There was only one explanation that made any sense. He looked at her face, so close to his. "You're a virgin, aren't you?" he asked abruptly. Of course she was! Someone so young, with such angelic innocence burning in her eyes...no one would have dared to taint such beauty.

She nodded. "The creature leaves my tribe alone if we offer up a virgin each year."

He sighed. "Bastards. Where are they?" He hadn't seen any sign of habitation. There didn't seem to be anything in this world other than rock, clouds and sky.

"We live below ground, in caves," she said. "The creature's limbs come down to our caves if a sacrifice is not offered, and rape indiscriminately."

He looked up at the tentacles still roving aimlessly, questing about blindly for the girl. Those massive phalluses had gone soft. The tentacles passed directly above his head occasionally, and he feared they might accidentally brush against him or her, discovering both him and the girl. He had no doubt they would be able to touch him, even though he seemed invisible to them. After all, he was solid enough to the girl. But why could she see him, but the tentacles couldn't? And...were they all part of the same creature, or were there many of them?

And too...how innocent could the girl actually be,

since she was obviously unwilling to sacrifice herself for her tribe? That wasn't a pure act. It was a selfish act.

"Would your tribe take you back?" he asked her. "Can we go to them?"

She shook her head vehemently. "They would stone me to death, and you for helping me."

He looked around the landscape. Where could he take her that was safe?

She said, "There is one certain way to protect me from the monster." He felt her hands fumbling with his pants, trying to get at his manhood.

"No," he hissed at her. He slapped her questing hands away. Doing so unbalanced him, and his full weight bore down upon her once again. She huffed as the breath was again knocked out of her.

"Are you sure?" she said. "Then we would have only my tribe to contend with."

"I'm sure," he said, looking down at her sweet face, which was the very ideal of beauty incarnate. "Please don't tempt me."

The thought of destroying her purity repelled him. He would not become a destroyer of innocence. But this all felt so unreal. He'd climbed upward toward the sky of one world, and had emerged from the ground of another. A world with some sort of monstrous creature prowling the sky, with phallus-tipped tentacles intent upon deflowering the girl. It was ridiculous and impossible, and...

He felt her hand fumbling again. But she couldn't seem to figure out how to undo his pants. Perhaps her people wore a different sort of clothing, or no clothing at all. Or, more than likely, she simply had no experience in undressing a man.

"Please don't tempt me," he repeated, imploring.

And then his mind made a connection. He'd entered another world! He recalled the poem in the painting. Something about a wind that blew across four worlds and a scattered girl... "You're her, aren't you?" he asked, his heart suddenly pounding. "You don't look like her, but somehow you are." He raised his face and shouted at the sky, "Is this all some kind of test? Are you testing me?"

"Who?" the girl asked.

"The woman in the painting."

"What? What's a painting?" She wrinkled her nose in confusion.

Then he remembered the gnarled oak tree, and the hobo code, and smiled. "I've got to take you back home," he told her. "Will you trust me? Will you come back with me?"

Her hand ceased its fumbling. "Wherever you go, I will follow."

"Good." Even as he had been speaking to her, he had been keeping an eye on the tentacles. They had been moving away slowly, expanding their search. Would they eventually give up and go away? Even if they did, the moment he stood up and the girl came out from beneath the shelter of his body, she would again be visible to the creature watching from the sky, and the tentacles would resume their pursuit.

But there was no other choice. They would have to run for it. He wasn't even sure what they would be running toward. The mansion, or at least this world's version of it? Or something connected the mansion? He didn't know. But he had to trust the hobo code. It had not let him down yet.

He looked out across the barren landscape and pointed in the direction he wanted her to go. "We're going to run in that direction. You'll see a gnarled tree with a symbol on it, and maybe a house eventually."

"What's a house?" she asked.

For a moment he thought she was being deliberately obtuse, but then realized that, living in a cave as she claimed her people did, she probably had no concept of man-made surface structures.

"A building, something people would live in," he told her. But even the concept of a *building* was probably beyond her. He pointed to one of the large tumbles of boulders scattered across the otherwise bleak landscape. "Like one of those rock hills, except made of wood and stone and built by people."

She shook her head. "I don't know of any place like that nearby."

"Do you get to the surface much?"

"No," she admitted.

He pointed again. "Then just run in that direction. When I say 'Drop!' you drop to the ground and I'll hide you with my body again. Okay?"

She nodded.

"Okay. Go!" he urged her.

She wormed out from beneath him, then jumped to her feet and raced away. In an instant he was up and after her. He had difficulty keeping up with her as his feet threatened to slip out from beneath him on the slick rock. She didn't seem to be experiencing the same trouble; she was no doubt used to ambling about on the glossy rock.

He peered around wildly as he ran. Finally he

caught sight of the tentacles, high in the sky to the left. The tentacles were undulating downward from the clouds again, like a gaggle of airborne snakes pursuing them across the landscape, their phallus heads swelling to full mast as they drew ever closer to their prey.

He continued running, trying to get as far as he could before calling an emergency stop. He huffed and puffed with exertion, not realizing that he'd run this far when he'd first heard the girl's scream and raced to find her.

Peering ahead, he searched for the landmark gnarled oak, worried that they were off course. But he found it, far ahead. Their course was true.

Above, the roiling dark clouds parted, and the monstrous eye peered down. Its gaze was fastened on the girl. The tentacles drew nearer, their tips hugely erect.

"Drop!" he shouted. He needn't have worried that she was too far ahead to hear; this world was unnaturally quiet, and the slick rocky ground reflected his voice aptly. He was gratified when she dropped immediately to the ground and slid a short distance before coming to rest.

It took him a moment to reach her. By the time he did, the tentacles were almost upon her. Reaching her, he threw himself down upon her, matching her position precisely so that she should be completely hidden from the sky creature.

And apparently she was. The tentacles hovered over the spot where she lay hidden. They swayed gently to random muscle contractions as if swaying in a slight breeze. They seemed confused.

He looked skyward, fearful of even locking gazes

with the sky beast. But he risked it. That enormous eye peered intently at him or, as he prayed was the correct interpretation, at the spot where the girl had seemingly vanished.

The tips of the tentacles slowly wilted. The eye in the sky peered elsewhere, here and there, searching the landscape. The clouds drifted over the eye once more, obscuring it, and the tentacles withdrew, retracting skyward.

He heaved a deep sigh. They'd avoided the creature once more. But their luck couldn't hold. Surely next time the creature would probe the spot where the girl disappeared, rather than settling for a visual scan. If it probed, it would find, and the girl was done for.

He didn't voice his worry. He lay atop the girl, both of them panting from their exertion, and decided that a new tactic was needed. He had an idea. But they would need a more comfortable hiding spot, one that would allow them more freedom of movement.

He peered around the nearby landscape. A dark opening in a nearby outcropping of rock beckoned to him. It might be the entrance to a cave. The outcropping was slightly off course, but it was closer than anything else. The gnarled oak and its own outcropping were still a considerable distance ahead. He wondered at that. Had he really run that far to find the girl? Or were distances somehow different, changing, in this world?

He shrugged; idle speculation was pointless. Even if distances were the same here as in his own world, the site of the mansion was a considerable distance beyond the gnarled oak. Perhaps a deadly distance. He doubted their chances of making it without his new tactic.

He pointed over to the outcropping with the dark opening. "There," he said. "That looks like a cave entrance. We'll run that way next."

She didn't question his reasons. "But that," she said, "is one of the entrances to my home. It leads down to the caverns of my people. They will turn us away." She didn't sound at all eager to return home.

"Is the entrance guarded?" he asked her.

"No."

"Well, we're not going down," he said, "so maybe they won't even know we're there until we've been and gone. We'll be safe for a few minutes."

She made a wordless sound of uncertainty, but nothing more. He took that as agreement.

"Let's go," he said, easing himself off her.

The moment his weight was removed, she was up and running at breakneck pace. He jumped up and raced after her.

As he ran, a monstrous roar reverberated across the sky. He looked up, expecting to see that awful eye peering down, perhaps with a gigantic mouth below it this time, howling. But he saw only the black clouds like a storm about to break. The roar came again, and this time he was certain: it came from something hidden above the clouds.

He ran all the harder, chest heaving, legs pumping, now burning from a buildup of lactic acid. Ahead, he saw the girl slip into the cave entrance. Moments later, the rocky outcrop loomed large, and then he too hurtled past the stony threshold, into a dim cave like an anteroom into a larger chamber. At the back of the small cave, the black mouth of a tunnel led down into the earth.

The girl was leaning against an upthrust of glistening rock at the center of the cave. The shadows were thick here, but overcast light from the outside world provided ample light for their purposes.

Without preamble, not even pausing to catch his breath and calm his racing heart, he began removing his clothing.

The girl watched, light and shadow playing across her nudity. "Have you changed your mind, then? You intend to spoil me for the monster?"

"No." He shook his head as he stepped from his jeans and tossed them over to her. They landed at her feet, where she stared at them, not understanding. "Put those on. Quickly!" He yanked his shirt off over his head and tossed that to her as well. The Key in his breast pocket made a metallic tink as the shirt hit the ground. Seconds later, every last stitch of his clothing lay at her feet, and he stood as naked as she. The slick rock was cold against his bare feet, and a slight breeze from the depths of the earth wafted from the tunnel, chilling him, flash-drying the sweat that ran in rivulets down his skin.

"Put them on!" he urged her. Another roar came from outside, like a shrill blare from a horn.

She bent down, picked up his shirt, and pulled it down over her head. She grimaced as she adjusted it on her torso, obviously repelled by the sweat soaking it. The Key of the Ancients was visible as a dark outline through the breast pocket. She could surely feel the weight of the large key, but didn't investigate it. The shirt was much too large for her; it hung on her like a blanket, the sleeves coming down far past her hands, concealing them. That was a good thing, he hoped.

Then she put on the pants, which weren't quite as drenched with his bodily exudations, so didn't draw as much of a disgusted grimace from her pretty face. The pants were also too large, hiding her bare feet. "I can't walk in these, much less run," she told him.

"That's all right," he said, stepping toward her. "My clothing will protect you from the creature, like a cloak of invisibility." At least, such was his hope. If the creature couldn't see him because he wasn't of this world, neither was his clothing, so it should conceal her in the same way his body did. Theoretically it would work, but he didn't voice his doubts to her.

"El!" a voice shouted from the back of the cave. The girl whirled toward the voice, and Kurt whirled as well. He realized it was the first time he had heard the girl's name, nor had he yet told her his own.

A wizened, skinny old man emerged from the tunnel. He was dressed in a brown robe cinched at the waist, much like a monk. A thin, tangled gray goatee clung to his pointed chin, beneath parched lips, a sharp beak of a nose, and rheumy eyes whose corners were etched with thick wrinkles. A green teardrop was tattooed below the corner of his right eye.

"El!" he shouted again, stalking toward her. "I come up to go check to be sure the sacrifice is accepted, and what do I find? You! Here! Explain this outrage!"

Kurt stepped between the girl and the old man. "No! *You* explain the outrage of offering her for sacrifice to that monster!"

The old man drew up short, as if just now realizing El wasn't alone. "Who are you?" he asked.

"My name is Kurt," Kurt said, more for the girl's benefit than for the old man's. "Who are *you?*"

"I'm Daront, an elder of her tribe," the old man said. "What tribe are you with, Kurt?"

"I'm my own tribe," Kurt said.

The girl peeked out from behind Kurt. "Elder Daront, allow me to explain—"

"Yes!" Daront hissed. "Explain! Explain how you could betray your tribe this way. Explain how you could put yourself above the survival of your own tribe, of your own family! Explain what drives such selfishness!"

"But, Elder, I—"

"She doesn't need to explain her urge for self-preservation," Kurt interjected.

"Then you explain, sir!" Daront continued blasting out his fury. "Explain how you, a grown man, could interfere with the private affairs of another tribe! You may be an outcast, a tribe unto yourself, but even outcasts respect the Law of Sacrifice!"

"Eldest," the girl said meekly. "In my defense, I can only say that, as I lay upon the altar awaiting the beast, I came to realize that I did not wish to give myself to it, that I might burst and die even as I give life to its children, which would continue to terrorize the tribe. I began to think perhaps the cycle of sacrifice should be broken now. I cried out for help, and this man answered, as though sent by the ancient gods themselves. He delivered me from the beast, and I believe he is a sign from the gods that they wish us to end the sacrifices."

Daront drew back indignantly. "You are a mere child, not an elder. How dare you determine the fate of your own tribe, as if you are wise!" He opened his mouth as if to further berate her, but closed it without speaking. The anger drained from his face, as if he realized a different approach might work better. His face adopted a mask of compassion and reason. "Your mother, your father, El!" he implored. "Think of them! Think of your newborn brother. If you don't give yourself to the beast, it will decimate us. It will show no mercy. We cannot fight it, El. Please, I implore you, go out there and give yourself to the beast before it's too late!" He pointed at the cave entrance.

As if on cue, the blaring roar ripped the air for the first time in many long minutes. Kurt felt the girl pressing close against his back, trembling against him, clinging to the sole place of safety that remained for her in this world. He was her rock.

"Please, El," Daront said softly. "I can't believe the angel of our tribe would doom us all."

Kurt, who'd been keeping his eyes fastened warily upon Daront and the tunnel behind him, felt the pressure against his back disappear as Daront's words persuaded her. He heard shuffling footsteps behind him. He looked back and saw El trudging purposefully toward the cave entrance. "Tell my family—tell the tribe—that I loved them," she told Daront.

"El, no!" Kurt started toward her.

Daront grabbed Kurt's arm, restraining him with a grip that was surprisingly strong for someone so old.

Kurt whirled and slammed his knee up into Daront's crotch. The old man released Kurt and reeled backward, doubling over upon himself and retching.

At least Daront's stones hadn't yet shriveled with age like the rest of him.

"I'm sorry," Kurt told him. He whirled from the old man and raced to the cave entrance, where he swept El up in his arms. She squealed as he tossed her over his right shoulder and raced out of the cave.

She thrashed against him, pummeling his back with her small delicate hands. "Let me go! I have to give myself to the beast!"

He ignored her. Orienting himself upon the gnarled oak tree in the far distance, he ran for all he was worth. His bare feet slapped and slipped on the black rock. His manhood, unrestrained by fabric, jounced with every stride, slapping painfully back and forth from one thigh to another.

In the sky, the clouds parted and the humongous eye peered down, searching the landscape. Several times, its gaze swept across Kurt and his unwilling passenger, and passed on.

The tentacles descended and began thrashing against the ground, battering it as if the creature were throwing a tantrum, or was hoping to randomly smite its invisible prey. Kurt had to dodge and weave constantly as he ran. He jumped up and over tentacles; he ducked; he bobbed, he weaved. And all the while, El squirmed in his grip, struggling to free herself. But her efforts were in vain. He was much too strong for her. She screamed at him, she implored him, she called up to the sky beast to take her. But it seemed not to hear her, its tentacles alternately thrashing the ground and questing aimlessly

"Please let me go," she sobbed.

"I will not," he said. "I will save you, even if you

no longer wish it."

Eventually, long after he had passed the gnarled oak tree with its hobo symbol, a square enclosure loomed in the distance. As he drew nearer, it became obvious what it was: a walled garden of slick river stone, with a rusty iron gate hanging half off its hinges in a high archway.

It was the walled garden from the painting, the walled garden that sat in front of the mansion in his own world. But of the mansion there was no sign. Just the walled garden standing alone and forlorn in the barren, bleak landscape. Vegetation was visible through the gate and above the walls: rose blossoms, apples, clinging vines creeping across the top of the walls and down its sides. The colors were unusually vivid and vibrant against the uniform gray backdrop of this world. The fragrances of flowering life wafted on the breeze, caressing his nostrils.

At long last the tentacles seemed to somehow catch sight of Kurt and the girl. A triumphant blaring roar trumpeted across the sky. The tentacles swooped in from the sides and rear, their flaccid tips quickly springing erect. Kurt gritted his teeth and threw what little energy he had left into closing the distance to the garden. His legs pumped madly, and at any moment he feared he would slip on the slick ground and break his head open. He felt something hard and fleshy tap his left shoulder, felt something slimy brush against the nape of his neck. El screamed, splitting his eardrums.

And then he was racing through the half-open garden gate, in among the wild growth of plants.

He felt a sudden twisting somewhere deep in his bones, and in one blink of an eye he was racing back out of the garden. Sound and light exploded around him: the sounds of birds chirping and the hum of cricket, the light of the early evening sun shining low in a cloudless sky. Warm grass tickling his bare feet.

The weight of the girl abruptly vanished from his shoulder as soon as he passed the threshold of the garden back into his own world. His clothing that she'd been wearing fell limply upon his shoulders, suddenly empty of El.

He stopped running and dropped to the ground, his chest heaving as he gulped in great bursts of air.

He felt frantically at the empty clothing; his eyes searched for her through the garden gate. Had he dropped her within the garden during the passage back to his own world? No. She was simply gone. Gone! Had she been unable to pass through whatever barrier might separate the two worlds?

A sudden heat through the fabric of the shirt he was clutching caught his attention. He opened the breast pocket and pulled out the Key of the Ancients. Where before the bow had been a mere section of what had apparently once been a heart shape, there was now a new section, so that the bow now formed half a heart. Only half a heart. The new section was glowing red hot, as if the Key had just been pulled from a fiery forge.

He stared at the thing, his mind half beginning to grasp what was occurring. El hadn't vanished. She hadn't been left in that other world. She was here. He knew it with an uncanny certainty. There was no need to attempt to return to that other world to see if she'd been left behind, if such a return were even possible. She hadn't been. She hadn't.

The Key cooled until the new section was the same tarnished gold color as the rest of it. He clutched the Key in his fist and pressed it against his heart. Then he stood and, still clutching the Key reverently against his heart, walked into the house to retrieve a set of clean clothes from his backpack.

The Blank Woman

He walked into the library and immediately felt self-conscious at being naked in front of the woman in the painting. As he crossed the room to where his backpack sat beside the dusty chair, he stared sidelong at her. Her frozen, lascivious yet innocent smirk and frankly appraising gaze made his manhood stir.

"Do you like what you see?" he asked her.

He put the Key of the Ancients down on the table, then sat on the edge of the chair and pulled his last set of fresh clothing from his backpack. He would need to find a washing machine soon, or at least a place to manually wash his clothes.

He blushed as he donned his shirt. "I'm sorry," he told her. "I shouldn't have said that. And I shouldn't be proud to be naked in the presence of such a noble lady." He quickly pulled on his underwear, socks, and jeans.

Standing, he held up his arms and twirled completely around. "There. More presentable, I hope?"

He picked up the Key and held it aloft for her inspection. "I've got the Key of the Ancients, and I've got El. What's next?"

He waited for several long moments, listening carefully. Of course, he didn't expect the painting to respond vocally, but perhaps he might hear words in the distant sighing of wind, or a pattern in the usually random noises of the house settling. But he heard nothing, so he finally gave up and tucked the Key away in the breast pocket of his plaid flannel shirt. This was the fanciest shirt he owned at present; he reserved it for the rare occasions when people he met along the road invited him into their houses for a free meal, or drove him into town for a more formal dinner.

"Well," he told the painting, "I guess I'll have dinner now. It'll be dark soon, I suppose. I'll see you later."

He left the room, crossed the entrance hall to the dining room, and retrieved an MRE from the table. Figuring it would be a nice evening to eat outside, he took the packaged meal out to the porch, and seated himself on the rickety rocking chair he'd used upon his arrival the previous night. The previous night, which now seemed so long ago. In front of him, the sun was about to sink below the distant tree line. The sky over there was splattered with the beginnings of what promised to be a glorious sunset.

He ripped open the packaging and waited the amazingly brief time it took for the meal to heat itself. Then he tore into the bland yet edible meatloaf and potatoes. After the strange sojourn into that other world, he was ravenous and would have eaten just about anything.

Halfway through the meal, motion out on the lawn caught his attention and he looked up.

The mysterious gray woman in the perpetually bedraggled, wet clothing was shambling across the meadow toward the house, her movements slow, rigid and mechanical.

He put the meal down on the banister before him and stood.

She halted at his sudden motion, still halfway across the meadow.

He held his arms up, palms out, to show that he was unarmed and not a threat. Fearing that his voice would startle her into fleeing, he didn't speak. He stared at her. Why couldn't he see her face yet? She was close enough that he should have been able to discern her features, but her face was still fuzzy, vague.

After a long moment, she started forward again. He remained completely still as she approached.

Soon she reached the foot of the porch stairs, where she halted. Almost right on the spot where he had dug up the Key of the Ancients.

"Hello?" he said, keeping his voice soft. He waited to see if she would run from his voice. But she stayed. Just stood there. "I'm Kurt," he ventured again.

She stood there. But now, he was feeling that he himself might be the one to flee at any second. His skin was crawling, because the woman had no face.

Her skin was ghostly pale and slick with rivulets of water that ran down her body as if she were standing in some invisible storm. She was clad only a Victoria-era chemise and drawers that were plastered to her voluptuous body, soaked from the ghostly deluge. Her fiery red hair was likewise plastered to her head, framing a featureless plain of flesh where her face should have been. No nose, no eyes, no mouth, no cheekbones.

She was a blank woman, a lump of clay waiting for some sculptor to arrive and etch her a face.

He gulped. He fought his urge to flee. He told

himself that she couldn't mean him any harm. She wasn't the manifestation of some eldritch force come to drag him to his grave. Rather, she had something to do with the woman in the painting, and with El, with whatever unearthly situation he was caught up in. He wasn't caught up in evil; he was caught up in some sort of supernatural situation born from love.

He kept repeating that to himself, and slowly sat back down on the rickety chair. No longer hungry or able to eat, he left the MRE on the banister to grow cold.

He sat and stared at her until long after the sun had set and the nearly full moon rose to cast its silvery light upon the meadow and the mansion. And she simply stood there, dripping water onto the cobblestoned path at the foot of the porch, her blank 'face' turned toward him.

Could she somehow see him? Could she hear him?

Not if he didn't speak to her, she couldn't.

So he spoke, just to see if she would react. "Do you know why I'm here?" he asked her. When she didn't respond, he told her anyway. "I'm here because my life was a wreck. I've been directionless my whole life, stumbling aimlessly through the years without sticking to any sort of plan, until finally I hit forty and realized I was a complete failure at anything that had ever mattered to me. No family, no career, no love... I was a miserable failure, living in the ashes of my dreams. So I left it. One day I just became so sick of the mess I'd made for myself that I threw everything that mattered to me into a backpack and I left. I walked away, and I've been walking ever since, hoping to stumble into my destiny. And I'll keep walking until

I do, or until I die."

She abruptly turned and walked away, shambling back across the meadow. He watched her until she'd disappeared into the distant woods.

He felt a little miffed. He'd opened up to her, and she had just left without any sort of reaction to him. Or was the leaving itself a reaction, a rejection of him?

He walked over to the stairs and looked down at the ground where she'd been standing. There was no sign of the water that had been constantly streaming off her onto the ground. The old cobblestones overgrown with weeds were as dry as bone.

Lifting his gaze back to the distant tree line, he called out, "Come back soon!"

Then he went back into the mansion, where he lit several oil lamps throughout the place, and settled in for the night.

The Pond

The night was long and uneventful, a lonely stretch of darkness in which he listened to the sound of the wind sighing outside the house, and the far off, wooden creaks and groans of the house settling. As he had the previous night, he sat in the chair in the library, and by the flickering light of an oil lamp, gazed across the room at the portrait of the long dead or perhaps imaginary woman who had, for some bizarre reason he still could not quite fathom, captured his heart, until finally he fell asleep as the nearly full moon's silvery light seeped in around the edges of the drapes.

Later, he jerked spasmodically into consciousness with the groggy awareness that someone had loudly called out his name. Through the doorway across from him, he saw movement as someone or something just disappeared from view.

He jumped up and raced out into the entrance hall, looking to the right, toward the front door. The door was closed; he saw no one, no thing. Had he imagined he'd heard his name, the same way he was sometimes awakened by a single phantom bang? He'd been diagnosed with exploding head syndrome years earlier, so it could merely have been that which had awakened him. But the movement? It was now early morning, judging by the wan sunlight streaming in through the windows, so he couldn't have seen merely the flickering of shadows cast by the oil lamp. His imagination then, his still groggy mind playing tricks upon him?

No. The explanation was not so mundane. The spirit haunting this place had decided he'd slept long enough, and had manifested long enough to awaken him. The woman in the painting was impatient for him to complete the Key of the Ancients. After the events of yesterday, how could he have any doubts?

He cast a last look around the entrance hall. Still nothing. A search of the dining room revealed the same.

Figuring that the woman would at least give him long enough to eat a decent breakfast, he sorted through the MREs on the table, looking for something appropriate. But the meals were all dinner items, not breakfast.

Deciding to brave the skeleton in the pantry, he went into the kitchen and opened the pantry door. The skeleton still lay in deathly repose upon the floor precisely as he'd last seen it. At least *it* wasn't shambling about the house; he doubted if he could tolerate *that* level of supernatural behavior without breaking down into gibbering terror.

He located a meal labeled "Sausage and Eggs," which he took to the dining room and quickly consumed. Then he went out onto the porch, where he stood at the banister and surveyed the meadow.

The sky was a clear, cloudless blue. The grass glistened wetly with morning dew. A few birds wheeled overhead. The distant trees rustled in a light breeze.

There was no sign of the blank woman.

He thrummed his fingers on the banister's edge. What to do now? What was the next step in the puzzle?

He had climbed up the attic shaft and come out of the garden gate. Perhaps if he tried going the opposite direction? He went out to the garden and stepped through the gate.

Nothing happened. He merely passed inside, finding himself among a wild profusion of plant life that had been too long untended. He pushed his way through the growth to the back wall. From there, he struggled through the foliage, following the walls all the way around the garden and back to his starting point at the rear wall. He found nothing, no hidden doors, no loose stones, no passages to other dimensions.

He stepped back out of the garden and looked around. The house, the meadow, and the surrounding woods seemed unchanged.

The pond to the left of the house beckoned. Like the garden and the trap door in the closet, the pond was also featured in the painting's montage, so it must hold some significance.

He walked over to it and stood on its muddy shore. The pond was roughly ovular, about fifty feet at its widest point. The surface was utterly calm despite the soft breeze which stirred the grass along the banks. The lily pads and the green scum that covered the pond's surface were likewise unstirred by the breeze. The surface was a perfect mirror reflecting the sky and the clouds, tainted brown by the murk of the water's depths.

Kneeling, he thrust his hand into the water and groped for the ground. He found it when his arm had been submerged up to his elbow. His hand closed around a handful of the pond's muddy bottom, and he withdrew his arm. It came out with a coating of brownish-green slime, and the handful of muddy, dark soil sluiced away through his fingers like fine beach sand and dripped from the edge of his hand back down to the pond, where it struck the surface without causing the slightest ripple.

He shook his hand back and forth through the air to dry it. He resisted the urge to wipe the slime off onto his pants, since he couldn't afford to dirty his sole remaining pair of clean clothes.

At the same instant he was thinking of his clean clothes, he felt a pair of hands slap against his shoulder blades and shove, hard enough to knock him off balance. Screaming, he toppled forward, struck the surface of the pond, and sank into its depths. Complete darkness enfolded him as the daylight failed to penetrate even an inch beneath the surface. He instinctively closed his eyes against the fine, muddy grit that scraped against his eyeballs. He gulped in a few mouthfuls of water before he held his breath. He lashed out, trying to find the pond's floor with his feet and push himself to the surface. He found nothing! He shouldn't have even been able to sink; the water had only come up to his elbow before he'd found the bottom. Could the ground have sloped so sharply just a few feet beyond, so that he couldn't even find it?

He thrashed about wildly, tried to swim upward. But there was no light by which to orient himself, so for all he knew, he could still be sinking, or swimming deeper. And then something wrapped around his right ankle and tugged, yanking him in the direction he assumed was down, and he struggled all the more, but it was futile. The water and the dissolved sand rushed past him as he was dragged downward. He was buffeted by powerful currents, further twisting his already failing sense of direction. His chest burned, and he began struggling with the urge to open his mouth and gulp water into his lungs. He began to see sparks dancing in the darkness as his brain was depleted of oxygen. He felt himself going limp and growing numb, tugged downward, ever downward.

And then he erupted from the water, bobbing high like a surfacing diver. Light exploded against his closed eyelids, and he opened them. He gulped in huge breaths of air as his feet and hands suddenly found the pond's bottom. He half-crawled, half-dragged himself to the shore and heaved himself from the pond, and lay for several long moments, gasping for breath.

Thirst

Kurt lay there, for the moment aware only that the sun was incredibly bright, and the air was incredibly hot, so hot that he could feel the pond slime flash-drying on his skin, turning into a crusty, brittle shell encasing his body. Soon he could feel the ground baking his skin even through his wet clothing, making it apparent that even the ground was blistering hot.

So he thought it best to have a look around, and roused himself.

As he sat up, the shell of slime cracked and fell away from him. Looking around, he saw that he was still on the shores of a pond that appeared identical to the one he'd fallen into. But everything else had changed.

The Victorian mansion was gone. The meadow was gone, the surrounding woods was gone, the garden was gone.

This pond was the sole irregularity in the midst of a burning hot desert. As far as he could see in every direction stretched a barren plain so parched and burnt by the sun that the ground was cracked and brittle, and shimmering waves of heat rose from it, making him feel as if he were in an oven. The breeze blew hot across his skin. The mere act of breathing was like inhaling flames. Even the Key of the Ancients in his breast pocket was radiating its own heat against his chest.

There was nothing out there as far as he could see. No trees, no vegetation evolved to survive desert conditions. Just the endless desert, the pond and him. And a metal bucket sitting off to the side, a few dozen feet from the pond. The bucket would hold perhaps five gallons. It was so completely out of place that he knew it must be significant.

A closer examination of the pond revealed that it *was* slightly different from its counterpart in his own world: it was smaller, evaporating in the heat, and shrinking visibly even as he watched. The muddy shore flash-dried moments after it was exposed by the retreating waterline. At the rate the pond was shrinking, it would be gone within hours.

Even as he studied the pond, the water near the center began to bubble. Small bubbles at first, then bigger ones, which finally merged into one large bubble that grew and grew into a shimmering column of water that extruded from the surface, fountaining upward.

He slowly backed away, uncertain what was happening.

The column took on the form of a woman, a very voluptuous woman. The form was constantly flowing and breaking apart as water fell away from her, tugged back down to the pond by irresistible gravity. But generally the female form held a recognizable shape.

A woman formed from a fountain of water stood gazing at him from the center of the pond.

"The heat is consuming me," she said, her voice the whispering murmur of waves gently breaking upon a midnight shore. "Soon I will be no more. Take me home before it is too late." She pointed out into the desert. A shimmering curtain of water rained down from her extended arm, splashing noisily into the pond. "That way."

Without hesitation, he answered her, "I will!" How could he refuse her request? For this water woman was undoubtedly connected, somehow, to the Victorian woman in the painting. The woman with whom he had fallen in love. *Scattered by the wind that blows across four worlds...*

He had managed to memorize the short verse in the painting, having spent so much time staring at it.

"My name is Kurt," he told her, as if it would be of significance to her. "What is yours?" He wondered if her name would also be El.

"Nora," she said, her voice like the babbling of a brook.

Not El, then.

The woman pointed at the metal bucket nearby. "Bring it closer, please."

He did as she asked. The bucket had a metal handle that burned his hand as he picked it up. Gritting his teeth against the pain, he carried it to the shore of the evaporating pond and set it down. Then he backed away.

"Once I am in the bucket," she said, "I will not be able to reform until I am home. Until then, you will be alone."

"I understand," he said.

Without further word, the woman lost form, becoming once again a fountaining column of water. The column spurted high into the air, arcing over and down into the bucket. The bucket filled quickly. When it was nearly full, the fountain cut off. The last of the water arced through the air, filling the bucket up to the brim.

As soon as the bucket was full, the pond sank rapidly down into the ground, absorbed, until all that remained was a muddy depression which quickly flash-dried in the unbearable heat, becoming a stretch of cracked, parched ground indistinguishable from the surrounding desert.

"No!" he shouted plaintively. He needed some of that water to survive a desert trek! He also couldn't shake the feeling that the only doorway back home had just closed in his face.

He looked around at the bleak, inhospitable landscape. He looked up at the blistering sun. Then he looked at the large bucket of water. He was willing to wager that it was the only water he was likely to come across in this harsh land. Water he would desperately need before he found a way home.

But he couldn't drink it. He dared not. For it was *she*. She was a living creature dependent upon him to take her home before she evaporated. He couldn't even dip his shirt in the water to at least start out wet and fresh (his clothing had already dried from his recent immersion in the pond).

He licked his parched lips and squared his shoulders resolutely. Nothing for it but to get underway.

He picked up the bucket and he walked. And he walked. The sun didn't stray from its position at high noon, directly above him. It beat down upon him mercilessly, and it beat up on him mercilessly, reflected from the ground in shimmering waves of heat that were cooking him as surely as if he were in a convection oven. Though he was sure he must have been walking for hours, the sun didn't move a single degree, and it became clear: there would be no evening or night to bring respite from the skin- and lung-scorching heat.

Carrying the bucket turned every step into a struggle against both heat and gravity. Five gallons of water was no light burden, and he was forced to hold it in front of himself with both arms stretched downward as far as they would go, the weight of it hunching him over and forcing him to take slow, deliberate steps. His muscles strained painfully, and sweat squeezed from his pores until soon he had nothing left to sweat other than his own blood, which surely wouldn't be long in coming. On top of it all, his muscles, indeed his entire body, soon began to cramp.

His pace was so slow he expected to see a turtle go racing past at any moment. Given that he was beginning to feel light-headed and faint, he didn't doubt that he might truly begin to see such turtles, whether they were real or not. He couldn't be sure how fast he was actually going, for there were no landmarks against which to judge his progress.

Progress? He gave a manic laugh. Progress implied that one knew, or at least had an idea, how far the journey was from start to destination. But he had no idea where he was even going. He had nothing to gauge progress against, not even an idea. Just, "That way," as the woman had commanded. But was he even on course anymore? Had he been holding steady, or veered to the left or right of "that way"? Was her home at the edge of the desert, or somewhere in between? He could see nothing but flat, cracked desert land, and shimmering curtains of heat that obscured whatever might be on the distant horizon.

Occasionally, water sloshed over the sides of the bucket and splashed to the cracked ground, where it evaporated almost instantaneously. He grimaced at each lost drop. Was that a finger lost? A hand? A strand of red hair? An eye? He had to keep reminding himself that this was a woman in the bucket, not water. Her name was Nora. He began to whisper the name constantly, to remind himself, as thirst began to overwhelm him, wriggling its insistent bony fingers into every parched crevice of his body.

How long had he been walking? Hours? Days? His mind was burning up, and he stumbled on, becoming lost in a numbing fugue as rational thought slowly dribbled away, the sweat of an overheating brain.

He stumbled on a rock and fell to his knees, only just managing to keep himself from sprawling flat on his face by catching himself on the rim of the bucket. The bucket slammed to the ground as he did so, and a great wave of water sloshed over the side and splashed to the dry ground, lost.

He tried to cry out, "No!" but his throat was too dry, his vocal chords were too parched to make a sound, and his lips refused to open, as they had become fused together by a dry crustiness. He rubbed at them, trying to coax them apart, but it was painful, like rubbing sandpaper on an open wound. He reached down and rubbed a finger across the last of the barely damp ground where the water—drops of Nora, he reminded himself—were still evaporating. Then he rubbed the finger across his lips. The infinitesimal moisture he'd gleaned was enough to allow him to open his mouth.

And then he was overcome by a sudden wave of irrationality where thought was swept away and only a mindless animal remained, an animal dying of thirst. He plunged his entire head down into the bucket and took in great gulps of water, re-hydrating his shriveling flesh. The water was cool against his skin, and when he at last pulled his head from the bucket, he relished the feel of dried skin suddenly heavy with an abundance of moisture. He imagined that he could actually feel his face expanding as water swelled back into shriveled cells.

Reason returned, thought returned, and he sobbed, aghast at what he had done.

He had failed her!

The bucket was still a good three-quarters full. But the ground around it was dark with spillage: wasted bits of her, of Nora. And inside him... He had squandered a part of her, all for a brief moment of refreshment that he could even now feel slipping away, as it was devoured by the relentless and cursed sun.

"No!" he screamed, finally able to give vent to his rage, his anguish, his disgust with himself. He had failed her!

How long was the journey? How long had he already been walking? Because if he broke down like this again, and again, by the time he reached his destination, wherever and whatever it might be, there would be nothing left but an empty bucket. And he knew he *would* break down again, because at heart he was just a selfish animal bent on his own survival, even at her expense. That much had just been proven.

He climbed to his feet, picked up the bucket, and slogged onward, bowed under its weight, a weight now slightly less due to his outburst. He muttered a prayer to whatever god might be listening in this hellish world. He prayed for the journey to be over quickly.

But apparently the god of this world was not listening, for he walked. And he walked, and he walked some more. Surely hours had passed. Perhaps even days; the immobile sun offered no clue.

He succumbed to the animal three more times. Each time, he fought the urge to drink as long as he could. He fought until he thought he would manage to die before drinking. But eventually his survival instinct overcame his morality, and he dropped the bucket and plunged his head into the cool water, drinking until he could drink no more. And afterward, reason would return, and he would sob in shame.

After the third time, there would not be a fourth, because he had emptied the bucket. Nora was gone, absorbed into himself to slake his thirst, or wasted as spillage on the parched desert ground.

He had failed her. Finally and completely, he had failed her.

He left the bucket behind and continued walking. What else was there to do?

He wondered his failure hadn't automatically cast him back to his own world. Did that mean he was trapped here forever, or merely that he had to find the exit from this world, regardless of success or failure? The thought of being trapped here worried him. Since her home here offered the only possibility of escape from this brutal heat, he would find her home, or die trying. What else was there to do?

Now as he trudged along, he occasionally glanced behind himself to see how far he was from the bucket. He now had his landmark. It was lost to sight behind him surprisingly quickly, swallowed by the shimmering heat waves that danced on the horizon. At least the loss of the bucket proved that he was indeed moving across the desert; up until now, he had had no proof, since one spot of ground looked like any other.

Just when he thought he was on the verge of heat stroke, just when his skin was so fiery hot and red with a sunburn from which he would surely never recover, just when he would have been overwhelmed by the animal had he still possessed the bucket and Nora, he came to the foot of a sandy dune.

He stopped and looked at it in shock. It rose high above him, a frozen wave of fine, loose sand. He stooped and picked up a handful, to be sure he wasn't hallucinating. He let it trickle out through his fingers.

"Like sands in the hourglass, so go the days of our lives," he whispered deliriously, his voice cracking, his parched vocal chords burning with the effort of speech. "Or something like that."

The sandy slope ran to his left and right as far as he could see. He was happy to see it simply because it was something different. The unchanging barrenness of the desert had been broken. It had to mean he had reached some sort of milestone in his journey.

He climbed upward. With each step, his feet sank deeply into the loose sand, and the sand sucked at his feet as he tried to step further. For every foot progressed up the slope, he fell back half a foot, dragged by loose sand that slid downward.

But eventually he crested the dune, and stopped,

gaping in astonishment.

Surrounded on all sides by the endless desert was a grassy meadow, a narrow circle of life within the vast scorching emptiness. And at the center of the meadow was a sprawling Victorian mansion. *His* mansion. *Her* mansion.

And he knew: he had arrived at his destination.

Summoning up the last of his energy, he ran forward. He ran across the meadow to the pond at the side of the house and splashed into the stagnant water. He tried to dive, hoping to get lost in the shadowy depths and resurface again in his own world.

But he couldn't go deeper. The pond was only about a foot deep. He splashed around the entire area of the pond, searching for a less shallow spot, but found nothing.

He would not be going home through the pond.

Giving up, he lay at the center of the pond for a good long while like a hippopotamus, relishing the feel of the turbid water soaking deep into his parched skin. He dared not take a drink; despite his overwhelming thirst, he didn't want some sort of microbial amoeba or algal spore burrowing into his innards and wreaking havoc. Not even his animal instinct for survival could overwhelm him now; he was at least halfway home, and he was at least partially refreshed by the water and the greenery around him.

As he lazed in the water, he gradually became aware that he was being watched. He looked at the mansion.

On the porch stood a tall man dressed in green and brown Army camouflage khakis, watching Kurt.

As soon as Kurt noticed the man, the man

retreated into the mansion.

Kurt jumped up and splashed to the shore of the pond, then raced to the mansion in pursuit as fast as his water-soaked, leaden clothing would allow. Up the stairs to the porch, a quick glance toward the left to note the same rickety rocking chair he had slept in when he'd first arrived, the same broken glass littering the porch floor from the broken window. In the open door, and then WHAM! Something hard smacked him upside the head and everything went black.

But only for a moment. What could only have been seconds later, he came to his senses, finding himself on hands and knees on the floor of the entrance hall, dripping water into the layer of caked dust. His vision and balance reeled drunkenly as the man in Army khakis stood over him, wielding a heavy-duty iron frying pan in a white-knuckled grip. Kurt noticed that the man had a tattoo of a green teardrop at the corner of his right eye.

"Where is she?" the man shouted, spittle flying.

Kurt tried to rise, but the man waved the frying pan in warning.

"Where is she?" he shouted again.

Kurt worked his lips for several moments before he managed to croak out, "Who?" He put a hand to the back of his head. There was already a nasty lump at the base of his skull, but at least his hand came away bloodless.

"Don't play dumb with me!" the man shouted.

Kurt looked around the entrance hall, with no idea what he was searching for; just desperately casting his eyes about to see what weapons or opportunities were available with which to combat his assailant. The entrance hall was the same as it had been in his own world. He even noted a set of footprints in the dust and leaves coating the floor, footprints leading into the library to the left. They were about his size. Had he already returned to his own world, then?

The only thing out of the ordinary was a large bucket on the floor next to the door into the dining room. It looked like the same sort of bucket he had used to carry Nora before he'd—before he'd failed her.

The man in khakis noticed Kurt's eyes on the bucket.

"That's right," the man said. "Where is she?"

"Nora?"

"Nora." Keeping a wary eye on Kurt, the man reached out with a foot and knocked the bucket over. "Mine's empty. Couldn't get back home. Been here for weeks. She evaporated while I was waiting, searching for the way back." He waved the frying pan again, feinting at Kurt, who winced. "Where's yours? Give her to me so I can leave this place!" he shouted.

Kurt choked back a sob. "I drank her." He hung his head in shame.

The man's face twisted in a rictus of outrage. "You drank her? You drank her? You fucking *drank* her? Aaagh!" He drew his arm back, then swung forward. The frying pan slammed into the right side of Kurt's head, sending him reeling backward onto his heels and then over onto his back.

Fighting to keep from blacking out, Kurt coiled his legs in close to his chest and then kicked out. His feet connected with the enraged man's waist, doubling the man over and sending him stumbling backward into the dining room, arms cartwheeling as he tried to keep his balance.

Kurt used the momentum of his kick to lever himself up onto his feet. He rushed into the dining room after the man, figuring his only hope was a full assault rather than a retreat.

The man had fallen onto his backside in the middle of the dining room, losing his grip on the frying pan in the process. Kurt swept up a chair and raised it above his head, intending to break it over the man's head. But the man scrambled backward on hands and feet in a crab-like shuffle, narrowly avoiding the blow which Kurt was unable to halt. The chair struck the hardwood floor, painfully jarring Kurt's arms and shoulders.

Meanwhile, the man gained his feet and retreated into the kitchen.

Kurt picked up the frying pan the man had left behind. Wielding it like a sword, he faced the darkened doorway to kitchen. "I don't want to fight you!" he shouted. "*You* attacked *me!* Let's call a truce!"

"You fucking drank her!" came the man's shout from somewhere inside the kitchen.

"And you apparently didn't," Kurt said. "I'm not sure what's going on here, but one of us obviously did the wrong thing. I thought I did, but if you came before me and you managed to get her here, then maybe it was you, since you're still trapped in this world."

"Fuck you!"

"If I put down the frying pan," Kurt said, "can we try to talk like reasonable adults? Maybe we can help each other. Maybe we can help *her.*"

In answer, the man came rushing from the kitchen with a butcher knife raised above his head and a snarl on his lips. "She's mine, and I'll be damned if I'll share her!" He rushed at Kurt, the knife swinging downward.

Kurt threw up the frying pan and managed to catch the blow and push it aside. Momentum carried the man forward, and Kurt aided the process by stepping to one side and shoving against the man's back, sending him face first into the hard surface of the dining table.

Unfazed and in the same motion, the man whirled and raised the butcher knife again, tensing to rush Kurt a second time.

Kurt retreated into the kitchen. To his left, the pantry door hung open. To his right, below the sink, a drawer filled with knives was open. But Kurt didn't dare go for one, not with the enraged man hard on his heels. Instead, he swung around like a dervish, bringing the pan upward. His pirouette was effective, packing an immense wallop behind the pan, which caught the side of the man's head even as the man was nearly upon Kurt. The man was knocked sideways and into the doorway of the pantry, where he stood, shaking his head to clear it from the impact of the frying pan.

Not wasting a second, not wasting the man's hesitation, Kurt dove for the open drawer, yanked out a wickedly sharp knife, whirled, and sent the knife whizzing across the kitchen, where it sank into the man's chest with a horrifying squish of blood and gristle.

The man gurgled, and dropped his own knife to

clutch at the one in his chest. He stumbled backward, his astonished eyes glazing over with death as he toppled into the pantry. He hit the pantry floor and his flesh exploded in a powdery shower that rained down upon a collection of bones within camouflage khakis. The skeletal mess was in the same position as the bones in the pantry in Kurt's own world.

With a sudden intuition, he raced into the dining room, through the entrance hall and out onto the porch, to scan the environs. The surrounding desert was gone. The distant woods had returned. The sun was low above the trees to the west.

He was back in his own world!

But it was a joyless homecoming. He had just killed a man. He'd never taken a life. He felt sick to his stomach, and the sick rose up into his throat, the black bitter taste of bile, and he bent over and heaved a miniscule amount of it onto the porch. There wasn't much, since he had not eaten for who-knew how long, and hadn't drank for a while either. Once the trickling flow of bile ceased, the dry heaves continued to wrack him for several long moments.

When the heaves subsided, he leaned against the banister and took long, deep breaths, trying to calm himself and bundle the killing away into a dark recess of his mind.

"I'm back," he whispered to himself. "It was all for her. It was for Nora. Maybe it wasn't real to begin with. Just a test, that has to be it. I didn't kill anyone."

He kept repeating that to himself until he half-believed it. He had to, to keep the guilt from overwhelming him.

"It wasn't real. I'm back."

He patted his breast pocket and felt the reassuring solidity of the Key of the Ancients. He pulled it out. The heart on the bow was now three-quarters complete.

He sighed gratefully. He hadn't failed after all. She had sustained him, become a part of him. That other man had just let her evaporate. Kurt hadn't failed, and he was back. And he had brought her back with him.

El. And now Nora. One more piece to the Key, and...

...and what? What was this whole unbelievable situation building up to?

He clutched the Key to his heart, then tucked it back into his breast pocket and went back into the house.

Cared For

He went into the dining room and picked up an MRE from the jumbled pile he had placed on the table earlier. He was glad he'd put them there; he doubted he'd be able to face the skeleton in the closet for a good long while.

As soon as he settled into the chair, a wave of exhaustion swept over him. How long had it been since he'd slept? How long had he been in the desert? Hours? Days? He'd simply been walking and walking, unable to sleep in the heat. It surprised him now that he hadn't simply collapsed in the desert, delirious and exhausted, and died of a heat stroke.

But now that he was seated, the lack of sleep caught up with him in one fell swoop. He could barely muster the strength to tear open a meal labeled "Pork and Beans." It was even more work shoveling the bland food into his mouth. But he forced himself. He had to re-nourish his body.

As he chewed, he decided he should be grateful for the exhaustion. At least it masked the horrendous sunburn he'd acquired in the desert. He imagined that if he looked closely at himself in the mirror in the entrance hall, he would see a red devil staring back at him. If he hadn't been close to collapse from exhaustion, he had no doubt he would have been howling in pain. The soaking he'd recently gotten in the pond had been a blessing at first, but now his skin had mostly dried, and was beginning to crack and blister.

When he'd finished eating, he stood and stripped off his clothing, letting it drop to the dining room floor. The clothing was still damp, but soon it would be dry and would irritate and further inflame his skin. Nude, he shambled across the entrance hall and into the library to stand in front of the painting.

"I'll be upstairs if you need me," he told the woman. He'd decided that he needed a good amount of sleep in a real bed. He hadn't slept in a bed in weeks, not since a farmer had kindly allowed him to stay a night in the bed of his son, who had been away at college.

He felt reluctant to sleep anywhere but in the chair over by the window, where he and the woman in the painting could keep an eye on each other. But he'd seen beds during his earlier exploration of the mansion, and his exhausted body was demanding that he use one.

"My clothes and the Key are in the dining room," he told her. "Sorry, but I just can't do any more to help you right now. Give me a day or two to recover."

He shambled out of the library and climbed the grand staircase in the entrance hall. On the second floor, he found a bedroom with an antique four-poster bed and toppled onto the mattress with an ecstatic sigh. A massive plume of dust puffed into the air at his impact. He coughed briefly, but otherwise ignored the dust and the musty smell.

He fell instantly asleep.

For an unknown time, he lay there, drifting in and

out of sleep. A fever seized him, and a fog shrouded his numbed mind. His head ached terribly. He was too weak and sick to rise when he was awake, and too tired to dream when he was asleep. At least he thought he didn't dream. Once, drifting on the border of sleep and wakefulness, he was vaguely aware of a shadowy figure sitting on the edge of the bed, rubbing a cold gel, probably a salve of some kind, all over his naked skin. He couldn't even summon the energy to be frightened, and when he caught a brief glimpse of her face, he realized he had no reason to be scared: it was the blank woman, she with no face. But he couldn't be sure he wasn't dreaming her.

Over the hours or days, however long he lay there, he gradually recovered. After a period of time, he simply swam up out of the delirium to find himself returned to health. Looking back over the ordeal he'd been through, he wondered if he hadn't had a delayed heat stroke from his journey in the desert.

Recovered, he lazed in the bed for a long time, listening to the silence of the house. There was no light seeping in around the curtains of the only window in the room, so he figured it was night. Night of the same day he'd returned, he wondered? Or had he been bedridden for longer? It felt longer. He had the uncomfortable feeling that he'd been lying here for days, on the verge of death.

Looking down along the length of his naked body, he noted that the sunburn had faded from his skin, and it was no longer dry and cracking. Days, then. Possibly a week.

Then he realized that the room was dimly lit, even though no light came in through the curtains. That's when he realized there was an oil lamp flickering on the night stand beside the bed. Next to the oil lamp were the remains of several MREs.

Someone had lit the lamp, and someone had obviously been feeding him, though he had no memory of eating.

The blank woman!

He hadn't dreamed her after all.

She'd been caring for him.

Even as he thought of her, she came shuffling into the room. She stopped just inside the doorway, her faceless head turned toward him as if she could see him despite her lack of eyes.

"Good...evening?" he said, not sure it was evening, or early morning, for that matter.

But she didn't respond. She just stood there, a gray apparition that would have sent him into terrified hysterics at any other time in his life.

But not now. She was a part of whatever was playing out here. As was he.

He sat up on his elbows and studied her. Water still sluiced down her body as if she were standing in the midst of a rainstorm. It dripped from her body in a constant stream that somehow never made it to the floor. He wondered if she was capable of intercourse. Might that be why she had come now? The voluptuousness of her body, wonderfully visible beneath the nightclothes plastered wetly to her pale gray skin, clearly possessed the necessary organs for passion. He was naked, in bed... Had they already copulated? In his delirium, had he himself been capable enough to perform, a beast running on instinct just as he had been in the desert? Driven by unconscious lust rather than thirst?

He doubted it.

After long moments of staring at the featureless landscape of her smooth face, growing ever more disturbed by the sensation that she was staring right back at him, she suddenly lifted her left arm and pointed out the door.

She waited a moment, saying nothing, then lowered her arm and shambled out the door.

Obviously he was supposed to get up and follow.

He did so.

But when he got out into the hall, she had vanished. It had taken him a mere instant to exit the room, but in that split second of time, she had vanished.

The floor creaked in the eerie silence of night...or early morning?...as he went to the stairs and descended. In the entrance hall, the front door stood wide open, and he could see that it was definitely night. The deepest night, for the sky was strewn with thousands of stars, with no hint either of recent sunset or approaching dawn.

His clothing was undisturbed where he had left it on the dining room floor. He checked on the Key, confirming it was still in the breast pocket and three-quarters complete, then dressed and went out onto the porch.

He stood at the top of the stairs, surveying the meadow. Nothing seemed out of the ordinary. And there was no sign of the blank woman.

The silence was peaceful. It was so silent, in fact, that he almost imagined he could hear the stars tinkling high in the sky.

As he stood there, silvery light slowly crept across the landscape from behind the mansion. He stepped down from under the porch, walked a short distance out along the cobblestone pathway, and then and turned around to look upward.

The moon was just beginning to rise above the distant line of trees behind the house. It was a full moon. The gray pockmarked orb loomed close, casting its silvery reflected light down upon the mansion and the meadow.

And as the full moon rose higher, something strange occurred. Like invisible ink fading into view on a piece of paper, a narrow dirt lane slowly faded into existence a short distance from the mansion, as if being revealed by the full moon's light. The lane ran from east to west. The cobblestone path that had previously led from the stairs to a vague spot in the meadow now ran to the lane.

Warriors

Kurt stared at the road, awed. What would happen now? Perhaps a ghostly stagecoach would come trundling along the lane, and stop at the cobblestone pathway to call upon the residents of the mansion?

He walked down the pathway to stand beside the dirt lane. There were indeed well worn ruts near the center of the lane, skinny ruts like those that would be made by the wheels of a stagecoach. This was a well-traveled road, then.

He peered to his left, eastward. The distant line of trees, which had previously made an unbroken wall around the entire meadow, was now notched where the lane emerged from the woods.

Then he peered to his right, to where the advancing line of silvery light cast by the rising full moon was just now reaching the trees. Even as he watched, the moonlight touched those trees, and a gap gradually appeared as trees faded away, a gap through which the lane entered the woods.

He stood there for a long time, wondering what he was supposed to do, waiting for some clue. Waiting for that ghostly stagecoach, or perhaps someone to come wandering up the road. As he waited, the moon reached its zenith and started its journey toward the western horizon.

He shuffled his feet. His back was beginning to

ache from standing for so long. The night was chilly as well, making him doubly uncomfortable.

Then finally: movement to the west, where the lane led into the woods. Just flicker of movement at the corner of his eye that was gone by the time he turned his full attention upon it. The blank woman, or something else?

Well, he was tired of waiting. The movement was enough of a sign for him. He stepped onto the road and headed west. He reached the distant line of trees and passed into the woods. Tangled bushes grew on the embankments to either side, and branches arced out over the lane, so that he was almost walking in a sort of woodsy tunnel.

Sounds emanated from the forest: the crunching of twigs as unseen beasts prowled the night, the hooting of owls, and the chirruping of crickets. Pinpoints of light sometimes lit the murky depths of the woods, and he imagined they were the eyes of beasts watching him from the shadows.

Eventually he thought to look back the way he had come. When he did so, he discovered that the woods had closed in behind him. Behind him, the narrow lane led up to a wall of trees and just stopped.

Alarmed, he turned back the way he had been heading, and was doubly alarmed to find that the lane now ran only a few dozen feet further before dead-ending at a similar wall of trees. And even as he watched, the lane ahead of him gradually faded from view just as it had so recently faded *into* view, and as it faded, trees sprang up, closing the natural tunnel through which the lane had run.

He spun around in circles, watching as the lane

shrank toward him from both directions until finally he was standing on the last remaining section of the lane. And then that too vanished, leaving him standing in the deep of the woods, alone and exposed in the late hours of the night.

He looked upward. Through a gap in the branches, he saw that the full moon had been obscured behind a thick bank of clouds. Indeed, the cloud cover was so extensive that he doubted the moon would reemerge at all before sunrise.

The light of the full moon had opened the way, and now the absence of that same light had closed the way. Once again, he was trapped in another world. At least he assumed it was another world. But what if it wasn't? Could he simply retrace his steps to the mansion? Or continue forward until his path crossed the road he had been traveling before the storm had diverted him to the mansion?

Before he could even consider his next course of action, all hell broke loose.

From all around came the sound of running feet, crashing through branches and leaves. He crouched, looking warily in all directions. Ululating war cries echoed through the woods.

And then two lines of women came running from the trees to his left and right. They were carrying spears, and were dressed in deerskin loincloths and brassieres and moccasins and nothing more, like some sort of near-naked prehistoric savages.

The two groups rushed toward each other, spears jutting rigidly out, obviously closing for battle.

And he was right in the middle.

Before he could move, the two groups slammed

together like crashing waves. Several women on both sides went down in the initial engagement, gored by spears from opposing warriors. And then spears were tossed aside, useless in such close quarters. Fists and kicking legs became the weapons of choice as the women pummeled each other, hammering at faces, kicking, biting, pulling hair, tackling, rolling across the ground.

He cringed from the brutal onslaught which raged around him, somehow leaving him untouched. He watched in horror as necks were snapped on both sides, and other warriors dropped, felled by skull-crushing blows. And all the while, the women on both sides kept up ululating cries of rage and defiance intended to strike fear and confusion into the hearts of the enemy.

When one side had clearly gotten the upper hand, several women from that faction broke away and ran toward him. They snatched him up and dragged him away from the site of the battle, deeper into the woods. And then he realized: they had been fighting over him. The thought horrified him. That brutal slaughter, such violence—all over him?

Why?

He tried to resist, to break away and flee, but there were too many, and they were too strong. At one time, perhaps as recent as earlier that very day, the thought of being dragged away by a group of half-naked women might have been highly attractive.

But he found that the reality was exactly the opposite.

A few minutes later they forced their way through a tangled and dense cluster of bushes, at the heart of which was a small clearing. A camp had been set up in the clearing. Tents made of deerskin squatted low to the ground. Fire pits with embers glowing among ashes dotted the ground.

There were a few women already in the camp, who looked up alertly, spears at the ready, as Kurt's captors brought him into the clearing. They relaxed when they recognized their comrades.

He was hustled to the center of the camp, where branches tied together with vines had been fashioned into a makeshift cage. He was restrained as one of the women unlocked a lock and unwound a chain securing the door. The door was then opened, and he was pushed inside. The door was closed behind him, the chain rattling as it was wound around the bars again and locked.

There was one other man in the cage, sleeping on a bedroll in the far corner. In the darkness, Kurt couldn't get a good look to be sure, but the man looked to be only in his late teens.

The women stood outside the cage, peering in at Kurt. They ran their eyes up and down his body in frank assessment.

"He's a bit old," one of them said. An obviously pretty woman, beneath the dirt smearing her face and the twigs tangling her black hair. "But he looks like good enough stock."

"I claim first mating with him," said another, a leggy red-head with pendulous breasts. She looked at him lustfully. Unlike any of the others, she wore a necklace of bones around her slender neck. He wondered if that meant she was the chief of the tribe.

"You know the rules," said a third woman. "We

have to get him off the preserve first. You can't make a claim until we're back to our own lands and we can fight over him among ourselves."

"Damn the rules," said the redhead. "I want him now. You lot have fought poorly, and we might not be able to keep him. I've not had a man in years, and I'm not trusting my next fuck to your fighting skills."

And then a wizened old man stepped from the shadows. There was a green teardrop tattooed on his wrinkled, leathery forehead. "No, Lea. You cannot have him. You didn't take part in the battle that captured him."

"Excuse me, Honored Observer," Lea retorted, "but that was because I was ordered to guard *you*. Surely you can make an exception."

He smiled. "Sure. Come visit me in my tent later and we will discuss an exception."

"I'm not desperate enough to use your shriveled old cock, Observer." She peered in through the branches of the cage to look closely at Kurt. "I will have this one, whatever it takes."

Kurt stared back at her. He recognized something in her. The red hair. Something in the eyes.

She was this world's connection to the woman in the painting.

She took a deep breath and turned back to the Honored Observer. "I've reconsidered. We will discuss things in your tent later."

She cast a last longing glance at Kurt, then stalked away toward the tangled bushes that hid the camp from the outside.

As soon as she had left, the other gathered women began muttering in protest.

"This isn't fair!"

"The rules can't be changed!"

"Honored Observer, I protest!"

The wizened old man waved off the protests. "Ladies, ladies! Lea will not have her exception. There can be no exceptions." He grinned around at them, a broken-toothed grin. "Just allow an old man, once this tribe's greatest bull, to finally have his time with the only one ever to refuse him. Please?"

The women leered in at Kurt for several long moments, then walked away.

Except for one, a heavyset, muscular and homely woman who paused briefly to comment to the Honored Observer. "Have your way with her this night, Honored Observer. For I intend to challenge her and take control of the clan once we return to our lands." She cast a smiling glance back at Kurt. "I will have you first," she vowed, and then waddled away into the night.

He sat down onto his haunches and looked around the camp. His mind wandered. What was he supposed to do here? The answer was obvious: he had to get Lea back to his own world. But how? He was in a cage, surrounded by savage warrior women with spears who seemed intent upon taking him back to their lands, wherever those were.

Shortly, the women who had been left behind to finish the battle returned to the camp. Many of them were bloody and bruised, and several were so severely wounded they had to be carried in by their sisters. The wounded were taken into various tents, presumably to have their wounds tended. The remaining women retired to their tents as well, apparently to sleep off their battle fatigue. So following a brief period of activity when the warriors returned from the battle, the camp settled into a quiet time where the only thing to be heard was the distant chittering of nocturnal animals in the woods, and the occasional rustling as one of the women within the tents shifted in her sleep.

Kurt just squatted on his haunches near one wall of the makeshift cage. He didn't even try to sleep; he was too wound up, and anyway, he had no intention of staying here. His goal was to get the woman—Lea—and return to his own world.

So he sat, and he watched, alert for any opportunity that might present itself.

And soon, his patience paid off.

From a tent near the edge of the camp, Lea emerged and stalked toward a nearby tent with a scowl of distaste on her face. Kurt assumed it must be the tent of the Honored Observer.

Kurt waved to her, but doubted that she would be able to see him in the darkness. There were campfires scattered around the cluster of tents, but most of them burned low, not casting much light. So when his first waves failed to catch her attention, he hissed several times.

The other occupant of the cage, who had remained sleeping since Kurt's arrival, began to stir. So Kurt stopped hissing, frustrated.

But he had caught Lea's attention, for she altered her course toward what he presumed to be the tent of the Honored Observer, and headed toward the cage instead.

She stopped in front of him and put a hand on the wooden bars between them. "What is it?" she whispered with a strange tenderness in her voice.

"Let me out of here," he implored her. "Come away with me, just you and I." He'd been thinking as he sat waiting. These women apparently had to share their men. He gathered that men were rare in this world, for some reason. She'd already expressed desire for him. So he'd decided that the best route would be to appeal to her selfishness, tempt her with having him all to herself. It felt a bit arrogant—as if he were some stupendous prize!—but it was all he had to convince her to help him.

She shook her head. "You and I, alone? That's forbidden! It's unnatural. No one woman should have a man all to herself." Her tone wasn't one of refusal, but rather reluctant consideration.

"Why?" he asked. "What happened that there are so few men?"

She smirked at him. "Surely you know history!" she chided. "Even a child knows such things!"

"Just pretend that I don't. Please."

"There was a nuclear war long ago," she said in a long-suffering tone, clearly annoyed at having to recite something that she felt should be known by any sane person. "Humanity was nearly wiped out. Certainly our civilization was destroyed. And something came out of the war. A mutation, so that only one child out of a million is born male. There are only about five hundred million humans left now. You do the math."

He did, and the implications staggered him. But at least these women weren't truly the savages that they resembled. They were survivors living in the ashes of a collapsed civilization.

"So when male children come of age or adult

males are discovered in hiding, they're put into preserves like this one, and all the clans come here to fight over them. The victors take the males back to their own lands." She looked around warily. "I will say no more. My sisters will become suspicious if they see me talking to you alone. I must go. But do not worry. I will convince the Honored Observer to let me have you first." She reached through the bars and stroked his cheek.

She started to turn, but he reached out and caught her arm. "Please," he implored again. "Let's go, right now, together. Just the two of us. You and I."

She turned back to him, being deliberately careful not to let herself out of his grip. She was actually trembling beneath his touch!

"I can't!" she said. "My sisters would hunt us down and kill me for my selfishness."

"They won't find us," he assured her.

"Why not?"

He pressed his face close to the wooden bars and pulled her close. He could feel the warmth radiating from her body. It dispelled the chill of the night. "What if I told you I can take you to a place where they will never find us? Where we can live out our lives, belonging to no one but each other?"

"There is such a place?" She was breathing heavily, gazing at him with hungry eyes.

"A huge house in a meadow," he said. "A library filled with books. Do you remember anything like this?" He searched her eyes, seeing if his words sparked a memory within her. He'd been wondering if any of these women—El, Nora, and now Lea—had any recollection of who they really were. Lea was the first he had had the presence of mind or the time to ask.

She shook her head. "No. But..." She reached through the bars and stroked his cheek again.

"But what?"

"Something about you seems so familiar. I don't know why, or how. I can remember every man I've ever met, since I've met so few. And you and I, we've never met. And yet..."

"You don't belong here," he told her. "I know it probably sounds strange and unbelievable, but this—" He waved his arms in a broad gesture that took in the camp and the wider surroundings "—this place isn't the real world. This isn't *your* world. For some reason, you just can't remember who you really are and where you're really from."

She pulled back. "You're mad!"

"No!" he hissed, as quietly as he could. "Trust me. *Please*, trust me. Let's run away together. Right now!"

She took another step backward as if about to run. But she paused, and looked warily from left to right.

Then she stepped forward and unlocked the door of the makeshift cage.

But she hesitated before unwinding the chain. "I don't think I can do this silently. My sisters will be alerted. So when the door is open, we'll run, as fast as we can. You'll have to lead, since only you know the way to the place you speak of. I'll follow."

Oh, God! he thought, suddenly panicked. He had no idea which way to go! During his capture and the subsequent flight where he'd been hustled through the dark of the woods, he had lost all sense of orientation relative to the mansion. If it even existed in this world.

But just getting out of this cage and fleeing with the woman was half the battle. He had to believe that the way home would be revealed no matter which direction he fled.

So he kept his ignorance secret, and nodded to her. "I'm ready."

She unwound the chain from around the door, being as quiet as possible. But inevitably, the chain rattled. The sound was overly loud in the silence of the night, but miraculously didn't disturb the kid slumbering behind him.

The camp, however, responded almost immediately.

From a guard hidden in the shadows of the bushes that surrounded the camp came a cry of alarm: "Man escaping!"

At nearly the same instant, such that it was difficult to determine whether it was the guard's cry or the rattle of the chain that had roused them, sounds of stirring came from within the scattered tents.

By the time heads were poking from behind tent flaps, he and Lea were nearly to the camp's border opposite the guard who had raised the alarm, a guard who was already racing across the camp in pursuit.

He plunged into the barrier of bushes. Ignoring the whipping branches and snagging thorns, he crashed his way through. He could hear Lea hard on his heels.

Once out of the bushes, he kept on running in a random direction. Trees whizzed past him. Fallen twigs and leaves crackled beneath his feet. Far behind, he could hear similar sounds as Lea's clan sisters pounded through the dark woods like hounds pursuing a fox.

If he didn't find the mansion, and quickly, he was certain the chase would end soon, and badly, with Lea's probable death and his own return into slavery. But as he ran, he wondered: how bad would it truly be, serving as a sexual slave to however many hundreds or thousands of women were in Lea's clan?

He put that thought from his mind, fixing the beautiful face of the woman from the painting in his mind.

Even in the darkness, something on the bole of a passing tree caught his eye. He stopped dead in his tracks and leaned in for a closer look.

A carved circle with an arrow pointing to the left.

The trusty hobo code!

He wanted to shout out in relieved delight, but he held his tongue. No point in giving the pursuers another way to track him and Lea.

"This way," he whispered back to Lea, and took a hard left. He deliberately pushed himself even harder, forcing his legs to carry him at a breakneck pace through the night-darkened woods.

They crashed through the woods for a good ten minutes. Just when he was beginning to wonder if they were off course, another hobo code flashed by on a tree: "This way," pointing straight ahead.

There were still sounds of pursuit behind them, but as time passed, the sounds grew more distant. Were they outpacing Lea's clan? He let a slender thread of hope filter into his heart.

But just at that moment, a group of women burst from the woods to their left and slightly behind, and raced in pursuit.

"Is that your clan?" he asked Lea, his question punctuated by huge gasps as his lungs struggled for breath to power his run.

She glanced behind them. She didn't seem nearly as winded as he was; she was a warrior, after all.

"They are not," she responded after a moment's examination. She must have good eyes, to see in the dim light of the night.

"That's just great," he mumbled.

Their new pursuers moved fast. Kurt, already winded, couldn't force himself to run any faster. It was all he could do to maintain his current pace, which he wouldn't be able to much longer. He was already faltering.

And then they broke from the trees into a large meadow. Under the dim light of the stars, he could make out a shadowy structure at the center: the mansion!

The sight of it gave him the incentive he needed to send a last burst of energy to his leg muscles. "Come on!" he shouted back at Lea. "We're almost there!"

Lea looked ahead as she ran. "That house? We'll be trapped."

"Trust me!" he told her.

They were approaching the mansion from the rear. Strange. He had walked into the west, and didn't think his captors had taken him so far east that he would have had to run so far westward to return to the mansion. Apparently distance and directions were scrambled in this world.

"Does this place look familiar to you?" he called back to her.

"It does not. Should it?"

"I don't know."

He raced up to the back door of the mansion. Would it be unlocked? He hadn't even tried the back door during his exploration of the mansion. He didn't think they'd be able to make it to the front. Already he could hear their pursuers trampling across the meadow behind them. They began calling out their ululating war cries in anticipation of Kurt's imminent capture.

At least he assumed that was why they were raising their cries. But just as the bulk of the mansion obscured his view to the west, he saw a group of women break from the woods that way and begin loping toward the mansion.

"It's my clan," Lea muttered.

Kurt swore. How was that possible? Lea's clan had been behind them!

There was going to be another battle.

He flew up the steps to the narrow porch, threw open the screen door, and wrenched the doorknob of the back door. It turned.

Unlocked! Thank heaven for small miracles!

He pushed inward, and the door swung open. He hurried inside, and moved aside to make way for Lea. Then he slammed the door shut and turned the lock, heaving a sigh of relief as the bolt *thunked* into place.

They were inside not a moment too soon.

Seconds after they had entered, shouts and the clash of weapons, the blows of fists against flesh, sounded from beyond the walls.

Once again, the battle over Kurt was engaged.

"That should keep them occupied for awhile," he said. He felt guilty. Women were fighting and possibly dying right outside. All over him. It was an absurd situation. Even if he surrendered, he knew they wouldn't stop. They still had to decide which clan would possess him.

"Preposterous," he muttered.

"What now?" Lea asked.

They were standing in a small foyer. A long hallway in front of them led to the entrance hall at the front of the house.

"Surely you don't intend us to remain inside this house?" she continued. "As soon as the battle is over, the victors will just break in, claim you and kill me."

Kurt considered. What now, indeed? They were still in Lea's world. Where was the portal home? Should he try the closet hatch? Maybe it would climb upward...maybe up into the cellar of the mansion in his own world? Was that where the stairs down to the hypothetical cellar led? It sort of made sense, but yet it didn't, not even in light of the twisted worlds he'd already visited.

The walled garden? But that was outside, in the midst of the battle.

He mentally ran through the montage in the painting, searching for a clue. But he couldn't recall anything besides the cellar steps, the closet hatch, the walled garden and the pond.

But...

...would there be a painting in the library of *this* otherworldly mansion that might offer a clue?

With sounds of the battle still raging beyond the walls, he led Lea forward through the hallway. They emerged into the entrance hall. To either side rose the wings of the grand staircase. Past that, to the left, was the entrance to the dining room. To the right, the library entrance.

He headed toward the right.

Just as he was about to enter the library, something on the lintel of the front door caught his eye.

Hobo code.

The arrow pointed straight ahead. Outside.

He stopped and looked at it. Outside? Into the battle?

But he had to trust the code.

He reached out and opened the front door.

Out in the meadow, women were scattered around in groups of two or three, locked in mortal hand-to-hand combat. Through their midst, the Honored Observer strode toward the mansion. He saw the door open, and scowled in at Kurt and Lea.

"I see you in there, Lea!" he shouted, his voice surprisingly strong and loud for one of his age. "You've continually spurned me! If I can't have you, no one will!" He raised his arms above his head and began muttering words Kurt couldn't make out across the distance.

He reached out and took Lea's hand. He nodded toward the meadow. "Let's go home."

She balked. "Out there? But you said we were going to a place my clan could not find us. Yet now you would walk straight into their arms. You *are* mad!"

He tugged at her. "Trust me. Please."

She let herself be pulled forward.

As soon as he crossed the threshold of the front door, the Honored Observer and the battling women vanished. The hand he was holding vanished as well, as did the body it belonged to.

He walked to the banister of the porch and stood

looking across the empty meadow. The stars twinkled high in the black vault of the sky, and the full moon was just disappearing below the western horizon.

He was back in his own world.

He pulled the Key of the Ancients from his breast pocket. The last segment of the bow was in place. Lea. The heart was whole once again.

The Key was complete.

Fresh From the Oven

This time when he returned back to his own world, there was no respite for him to determine his next course of action. As soon as he had pulled the Key from his pocket to verify that it was complete—it *was*—the blank woman emerged from the distant forest and came shambling across the meadow to stand mutely at the foot of the porch stairs.

"Well, hello, gorgeous," he said to her.

In response, she raised her right arm and pointed off to the side of the house. Then she began shuffling slowly in that direction.

So. Not even a brief respite to sleep away the rest of the night. But he doubted he would be able to get in a decent amount of sleep before dawn anyway. He was too excited.

He stepped from the porch and followed the blank woman.

He had a suspicion of where she was headed, and could have raced ahead of her—her pace was so slow!—but he didn't. Instead, he walked patiently alongside her, forcing himself to take tiny steps to match her pace.

"So," he asked conversationally. "The Key is complete. Am I finally going to get some answers as to what this has all been about? Are you and I—am I and the woman in the painting—finally going to meet?"

She turned her faceless head his direction, literally giving him an inscrutable look. After all, she had no face to read. Then she turned her head forward again.

"Still giving me the silent treatment, eh?" he said playfully. "Fine."

They reached the far end of the house, and turned the corner. The slanted doors beckoned, the doors down into...down into what? Not the cellar, as he'd first suspected on his earlier trip down the stairs. Down to their final destination, perhaps, whatever that might be?

The blank woman headed straight for the stairs at her snail's pace. Now he let himself hurry ahead of her, and reached down for the left door. It swung up and then over, where he let it slam onto the ground. The blackened maw into the ground beneath the house stood open.

As the blank woman arrived, he stepped to the side and motioned to the entrance. "Ladies first," he told her with a grin.

Without pausing, she stepped down into the dark tunnel. She didn't bend in the slightest; she simply kept her rigid upright posture and descended down the first flight without varying her slow shambling walk. Despite her lack of eyes, she negotiated the stairs easily, without losing her balance.

He followed her down. As the darkness of the slanted tunnel swallowed him and the dim square of moonlit night shining in through the open door receded above him, he realized he hadn't brought any light. He paused his descent and was about to open his mouth to tell her he was going back to the house for an oil lamp when a pale light flared forth from his breast pocket.

He reached into it and pulled out the Key. No longer shielded by his clothing, the glow it was emitting surrounded him and the blank girl in a small sphere of wan light, ample enough to light their way. Or *his* way, at least; she didn't seem to have trouble walking in darkness despite her lack of eyes.

He looked at the Key. It wasn't hot to the touch; it just glowed with a dim golden light. "What does this mean?" he called down to the blank woman. She, of course, gave no answer.

He stepped downward, reached the first landing, turned the corner, and started down the second flight of stone steps. He paused on the second landing. This was where his oil lamp had been blown out on his first trip down here, and he'd turned back. In fact, the lamp and the shattered glass from its bulb still littered the landing.

He looked down the third flight of stairs and considered. What if he was being led into a trap? He believed something positive was going to come of all this. He believed he was on the final leg of his journey to meet the woman in the painting. But what if he weren't? What if this was another ghost story with an unhappy or fatal ending? What if he were in a horror story rather than a love story? What if this were his last chance to turn back?

Already halfway down the third flight of stairs (at least, he assumed it was halfway; in the darkness, who could be sure?), the blank woman paused and turned to face him, as if sensing his hesitation. For a long moment, he looked down at her, at that horrific wall of blank flesh where a face should have been. Any sane man would flee from such a sight.

But he was not sane. He had not been sane for a very long time, he suspected. A sane man wouldn't have abandoned a life forty years in the making to wander aimlessly around the country.

The blank woman reached up toward him, holding out her hand.

That decided him. He was in this until the end. He stepped downward and grasped the hand. It was deathly cold, but comforting. He was almost shocked that he could actually touch her; until then, he supposed he had assumed she would be insubstantial to the touch, like a ghost. But no. She was solid, cold, more like a walking corpse than a ghost. And he could actually feel the rivulets of water from the phantom storm running down her arm and onto his hand.

They continued downward like that: she in the lead, one arm reaching back to hold hands with him. Had the tunnel been wide enough, he supposed they would have walked side by side, holding hands like two lovers as they descended into the earth.

The stairs continued for an interminable span. After the tenth landing and three hundred stairs, he stopped counting. Estimating half a foot for each stair, he figured they must be at least one hundred and fifty feet below ground, below the house. Who would dig such a shaft of stairs, and to what purpose? The number of bricks required was staggering for him to think about. Ancient red bricks, loose and crumbling, with dirt spilling out and roots dangling from gaps where the mortar had worn away. Water streamed down the walls in places, and ran down the stairs in rivulets, making the descent slick and slow and treacherous. The air grew stale, musty and oppressive, and he imagined that he was breathing in moldy spores with each breath, spores that would lodge in his lungs and spread questing fungoid fingers throughout his chest. The air grew increasingly warmer as well, uncomfortably warm, almost unbearably stifling.

When they had descended another ten flights— could have been twice as many; he'd stopped counting, after all—they reached the end of the stairs. Now, a sagging, brick-lined tunnel led toward a flickering light in the distance. Without pause, the blank woman stepped forward. He let himself be pulled after her.

After a short walk, they stepped out into a low-ceilinged, dank room about twelve feet square. There was nothing here, no furniture, no boxes or other detritus that one might find in the cellar of a house. Just four bare moldy brick walls and a few puddles of moldy water on the floor. The air was almost scorching hot, and each breath seared his lungs. It was like that infernal desert world all over again.

The heat seemed to be coming from the only thing of note in the entire room: a small, square, rusted iron hatch set in the wall opposite the entrance, like the door of an oven or kiln. Flickering white hot flames could be seen dancing beyond a narrow grate in the door.

The blank woman finally let go of his hand and pointed at the iron hatch.

He stepped up to it and bent low to examine it. The heat emanating from it was intense, so intense he felt like retreating. But he steeled himself. There was a handle on one side of the hatch.

Looking at the blank woman, who had shambled

to his side, he asked, "What am I supposed to do?" For the life of him, he couldn't imagine how a fiery oven figured into all this.

But of course she did not, *could* not, answer.

There was only one possible course of action: open the hatch.

He set the Key of the Ancients, his makeshift flashlight, on the floor and took off his shirt. He wrapped it around his hand as a shield from the hot metal, then squatted and reached for the handle. It turned easily, and he pulled outward, but the hatch wouldn't budge.

It was locked.

The Key! He laughed in elation at the sudden obviousness of it. All his work had been to complete a key to unlock this hatch!

He looked below the handle and found a keyhole. He hadn't noticed it before now because he hadn't been at an angle to see the flames through it. But it was there.

He picked up the Key and slid it into the keyhole. He turned. There was a click and a heavy *thunk* as a bolt slid back. Then the Key vanished in a flash of light. Thankfully the flames from the oven, the kiln, whatever this was, were now providing the light, so the sudden absence of the Key didn't plunge the room into darkness.

The hatch door, surprisingly thick, swung open on creaking hinges, revealing a raging inferno inside a long, narrow enclosure. A blast of heat washed over him. Just when he thought it couldn't possibly have gotten any hotter...

The realization hit him then: this was a special sort

of oven, a grisly sort. It was, in fact, an antique cremation chamber, something straight out of a Victorian funeral parlor.

The blank woman moved. She bent, trying to climb into the chamber.

"No!" he shouted. He reached for her, tried to pull her back. But she shook him off easily and threw him aside with a surprising force. He stumbled backward and fell flat on his rear end. By the time he managed to scramble back to his feet, she had climbed inside. He could see her in there, a shadowy figure crawling back into the raging inferno until she lay prostrate, the flames consuming her.

As he leaped forward shouting, "No!", the hatch door slammed shut.

Carefully he grabbed the handle with his shielded hand, turned, and yanked, but nothing happened. The hatch would not open.

He resisted the urge to pound against the hot metal and scream. He wanted to scream for her because she couldn't scream herself. But in the end he stopped himself, because a rational part of himself realized that this must be how things were meant to unfold. The events he had been through had all been leading up to the blank woman crawling in to be cremated. He had committed to this adventure, so he had to let it run its predestined course.

He leaned forward and peered through the grate, watching as the shadowy prostrate form within was consumed and reduced to a scattering of white ash.

He slumped back onto his heels, sobbing despite himself. Sweat from the intense heat ran in rivulets down his bare chest.

He waited.

The flames in the oven gradually died down. He wondered: had the cremation chamber been ignited when he'd completed the Key?

He waited some more.

He imagined that he must have waited hours.

Then, the hatch handle creaked as it turned. He looked up, watching it. The handle turned!

Someone—some *thing*?—was opening the hatch from the inside.

He began backing away.

The hatch door creaked open. Hands reached out to grasp the walls. Delicate, pale human hands. Feminine hands, seeking leverage to drag herself from the chamber.

He hurried forward to aid the woman.

She emerged head-first, a head from which fiery red hair fell like a waterfall.

He didn't get a good look at her until she was out and standing tall and splendid before him: the woman from the painting, completely nude and smiling at him like the Goddess of Love herself. She was even more beautiful than in the painting; her beauty was surely so much greater than a mortal artist could ever manage to capture. There was a wonderful familiarity to her gaze, as if he were a beloved friend returned after a long absence. It made his heart ache for her.

She held out her hand. "Good day, sir. My name is Eleanora Paley." She spoke in a delightfully aristocratic voice. "It is my pleasure to meet you, though I'm not entirely certain we have not met before."

He grinned widely. Eleanora! At last he had a name for the woman who had smitten him! A combination of the names of the women he'd encountered in those other worlds. Still grinning, but in keeping with her formality, he took her hand and bent slightly to bring it to his lips. He planted a brief, chaste kiss on the back of her hand. "I'm Kurt," he introduced himself.

When he lowered her hand, she didn't let go. Rather, she held onto it and, with that entrancingly innocent yet wanton smirk dancing at the edges of her full lips, allowed him to lead her back up the stairs to her mansion, where they began a long and happy life together.

The Beginning of the Story

One hundred and forty-one years earlier

"Done!" Karl said, his voice bursting with pride. He stepped back from the easel and rubbed his hands together like a master chef dusting off his hands after finishing a culinary marvel.

The Lady Eleanora let out her pent up breath and relaxed her posture. It had been dreadful, holding that pose for hour upon hour while Karl captured her in paint for all eternity. Not that the process hadn't been pleasant; her hours of immobility this afternoon had afforded her ample time to get to know this wonderful vagabond who had come calling upon her that very morning, offering to paint her portrait. Ample time to come to one inescapable conclusion: she had taken a powerful fancy to the man, and would be truly sad to see him strike off away down the road and out of her life.

She stepped away from the porch stairs and joined Karl on the other side of the easel, to survey his handiwork.

The portrait was exquisite!

"I declare, dear sir," she said, "this is fine work indeed! It shall hang in my parlor for all to see, proclaiming your talent for whomever crosses the threshold of Paley House!"

"It shall not be my artistry they admire when they gaze at this," Karl said, "but rather the artistry of God who created a marvel such as you."

"Sir, one more word and I shall blush!"

He smiled at her, then turned and began packing away his paint and brushes.

She laid a tentative hand on his arm. "Can I offer you a glass of lemonade before you go, sir? A sandwich, perhaps?" She simply could not bear the thought of him walking out of her life now that he had entered it.

She held her breath as she awaited his answer. Would he think her too forward? Most men shied away from aggressive women.

He looked up from the small box into which he was packing the tools of his trade. "Yes, ma'am. I do believe the items you have offered would be quite agreeable."

She smiled and hurried toward her mansion with as much haste as dignity and her lacy dress would allow. "Please, make yourself at home on the porch while I fetch things from the kitchen." She climbed the porch stairs and went inside, nearly tripping over the train of her dress. Why, she was as nervous as a schoolgirl!

She hurried around the kitchen, fixing a sandwich, then pouring a tall glass of lemonade with an ice cube from the icebox. The inclusion of the ice cube was perhaps a bit ostentatious, but she needed to show that she was a woman of some means. She intended to hook this lovely man, and it would help if he thought she was a widower with a fortune or two tucked away somewhere. Though surely the absence of servants at

Paley House would speak the truth: she was near the end of what little her dear, late husband had left her. Karl had happened upon her in the twilight of her good fortune. But with a man around the place once again, all was not lost! Paley House would return to prosperity.

She heard voices outside. Karl's voice, and another she knew all too well, and dreaded.

She left the glass of lemonade and the sandwich on the kitchen counter, and ran to the entrance hall. She crept to the tall window next to the door. Cracking the curtain a bit, she surreptitiously peered out.

A tall, heavyset man stood out in the meadow, halfway between her house and the distant woods. He hadn't come on the road; he never did. He haunted the woods surrounding her house, making his home in a secret part of the woods which neither she nor the sheriff had yet been able to locate. He was looking off to the side of the porch, making slow gestures of clearly evil intent, as though conjuring forth the arcane energies of higher dimensions. She pressed her face close to the window, craning her neck to peer to her right. Karl was there at the porch railing. Even as she watched, he gave a strangled gasp, clutched at his chest and stumbled backward into the old rocking chair. Felled by magic, victim of the madman who stalked her.

She whirled from the window and retreated into the mansion. In the main hallway, she snatched a rifle from where it hung on the wall, then returned to the front of her home.

She stood in the center of the entrance hall, rifle clutched low and level as she stared out the window at the man who, having dealt with Karl, was now approaching across the meadow. She fired a warning shot out the window, the glass shattering outward. The approaching man paused a moment as the bullet whistled past his ugly face just inches short of the green teardrop tattooed at the corner of his left eye. Then he flashed her a toothy grin and continued forward.

She ran to the door, yanked it open, raised the rifle and sighted down the barrel at him. "Go away, Mr. Darabonne, or as God is my witness, the next bullet will go right between your unholy eyes."

His smile faded, but he didn't halt. He came forward until he stood at the foot of the stairs. Next to the easel upon which her portrait sat, the paint still drying. He looked at it and rage boiled on his face.

Darabonne had been an officer in the civil war that had so recently rocked her adopted country. He'd been discharged when it was discovered that he was practicing sorcerous arts upon the battlefield, attempting to raise the dead and other more nefarious deeds of black magic. Although she had never witnessed his use of such powers, she'd never doubted the charges against him, for he had the repulsive air of someone who had seen and done things no mortal man should. He'd been trying to court her during the years after her husband's death, a death in which she was certain he had had a hand. Over the years, his attempts to seduce her had grown increasingly forceful and erratic. Now, it seemed, he had abandoned all pretense at civility and intended to take her against her will.

"You harlot!" he shouted at her. "I offer you my

full attention and affection, which you continually spurn. Then the moment I turn my back, you gravitate toward the first stranger who happens along!" He gestured to his left, and against her will, she glanced to her right to see Karl slumped in the rocking chair at the far end of the porch. His eyes were closed and a look of horror twisted his face. His chest neither rose nor fell, and his utter stillness was clearly the stillness of death.

"You belong to me!" Darabonne shouted. "Your friends are mine to destroy at my whim, as are you! If I cannot have you, no one shall!"

Her heart caught in her throat. She was wrong. Darabonne had no intention of taking her against her will. This time, he intended to destroy her for all other men.

He stood at the foot of the porch, glaring darkly up at her as he began muttering ancient words of arcane power that twisted the very air between them, sapping it of light. Thunder sounded overhead as dark storm clouds suddenly moved in, drawing across the sun like a shroud and cloaking the world in a leaden gray. The air around her began to crackle with eldritch energy. Her hackles raised in response, her hair lifted and spread out around her head in a static nimbus, and she felt the flesh of her face growing soft, her features beginning to flow like wax down the sides of a candle. She screamed, and her mind shattered. Borne upon the breast of a spectral wind, her soul scattered in three impossible directions, while a fourth sliver of her consciousness remained within her body but lost in a fog of amnesia, though enough sense remained within her to flee.

Darabonne didn't stop her as she brushed past him and fled screaming across the meadow. Her sight faded before she'd reached the distant woods, and her screams were cut off as her mouth fused together like a healing wound, and her throat closed. She slowed to a stumbling shamble, stepping carefully in a suddenly dark world. Even her mind was retreating into darkness, the amnesia spreading into the depths of her being.

As she entered the woods, the sky opened and unleashed a torrential downpour.

Behind her, Darabonne's mad laughter rang across the meadow for a brief time, until her flowing ears sealed themselves and melted away, cutting him off.

And for a long time, she remembered no more.

Made in the USA
Columbia, SC
28 November 2022

72053644R00072